"A humdinger!"   —*Saturday Review*

"An infectiously exciting open-air thriller."
          —*The New York Times Book Review*

"It is a real pleasure to read such a straightforward adventure yarn...filled with danger and action and told with clarity."   —*San Francisco Chronicle*

AGROUND
was originally published by
The Viking Press, Inc.

Also by Charles Williams

The Sailcloth Shroud

 Are there paperbound books you want but cannot find in your retail stores?

You can get any title in print in **POCKET BOOK** editions. Simply send retail price, local sales tax, if any, plus 25¢ to cover mailing and handling costs to:

MAIL SERVICE DEPARTMENT
POCKET BOOKS ● A Division of Simon & Schuster, Inc.
1 West 39th Street ● New York, New York 10018

Please send check or money order. We cannot be responsible for cash.   *Catalogue sent free on request.*

Titles in this series are also available at discounts in quantity lots for industrial or sales-promotional use. For details write our Special Projects Agency: The Benjamin Company, Inc., 485 Madison Avenue, New York, N.Y. 10022.

AGROUND

Charles Williams

PUBLISHED BY POCKET BOOKS NEW YORK

AGROUND

Viking Press edition published July, 1960
POCKET BOOK edition published October, 1971

A condensed version of this novel appeared in **Cosmopolitan.**

This POCKET BOOK edition includes every word
contained in the original, higher-priced edition. It is printed
from brand-new plates made from completely reset, clear, easy-to-read
type. POCKET BOOK editions are published by POCKET BOOKS, a division
of Simon & Schuster, Inc., 630 Fifth Avenue, New York, N.Y. 10020.
Trademarks registered in the United States and other countries.

AGROUND

1

They were down at Miami International between thunder showers at 3:40 p.m. Ingram, a big, flat-faced man with aloof gray eyes and an almost imperceptible limp, followed the other passengers out of the DC-6 into the steamy vacuum left behind by the departing squall. His leg had stiffened a little, as it always did when he had to sit still for very long, and he thrust the foot down savagely against the pull of tendons as taut as winched halyards. He checked through Immigration, and when he was cleared by Customs he waved off the porter with a curt shake of his head, carried the old suitcase out to the lower ramp, and took a taxi downtown to the La Perla, the shabby third-rate hotel he'd first checked into some fifteen days before and had used as a base of operations ever since. There was no mail for him. Well, it was too soon.

"You can have the same room, sir, if you'd like," the clerk said.

"All right," he replied indifferently. It commanded a view of a dank airwell, but was cheaper than the outside ones. He signed the registry card and rode the palsied elevator to the third floor. The operator, a bored worldling of nineteen, picked up the suitcase and preceded him down a corridor where flooring creaked beneath its eroded carpet.

The room was high-ceilinged and dim and passably clean, stamped with the drab monotony of all cheap hotel rooms and that air of being ready, with the same weary and impervious acquiescence, for sleep, assignation, or suicide. The bathroom with its old-fashioned tub was just to the left of the doorway. Beyond its corner the room widened to encompass a grayish and sway-backed slab of bed, a dresser marked with cigarette burns and the

7

bleached circular stains of old highball glasses, and, at the far end, beside the window looking into the airwell, a writing desk, on top of which were the telephone, a coin-operated radio, and a small lamp with a dime-store shade. It had begun to rain again. He could see it falling into the airwell beyond the parted slats of the venetian blind. Looks like the set for an art motion-picture, he thought; all we need is a Message and a couple of rats.

The youth deposited the suitcase on a luggage stand at the foot of the bed and switched on the air-conditioning unit installed in the lower half of the window. Ingram dropped a quarter in his hand. He let it lie there for an insulting half-second before he closed the fingers, and started to look up at Ingram with the bright insolence of the under-tipped, but collided with an imperturbable gray stare that changed his mind. "Thank you," he said hurriedly, and went out.

Ingram ran hot water into the tub and stripped, hanging his suit in the closet with the automatic neatness of a man accustomed to policing his own loneliness. After rinsing out the drip-dry shirt, he selected a wooden hanger for it and hooked it on the curtain rod. When he got into the tub, he stretched his legs out and put his hands on the knee of the left one, forcing it down against the pull of the tendons. Sweat stood out on his face. It was better, he thought. He'd got rid of the crutches a month ago, and then the cane, just before he'd come up from San Juan. In another month the limp would be gone entirely, and there'd be nothing left but the scar tissue. After a while he climbed from the tub, blotted himself as well as he could with the sleazy and undersized towels, and put on a pair of boxer shorts. The skin across the hard wedge of his back and shoulders and the flat planes of his face had a faint yellowish cast, the residue of old tan faded by weeks in the hospital. The slick, hairless whorls and splotches of scar tissue around his left hip and in back of his left leg still had an ugly look, and would probably never tan again. He made the futile gesture of running a comb through the intransigent nap of graying dark hair, and went out into the bedroom.

He broke the seal on the Haig & Haig pinch bottle he'd bought in Nassau, and poured a drink. He selected one of the thin cigars from the leather case in his suit, lighted it, and looked at his watch on the dresser. He'd better call Hollister and explain what he'd done. He was just reaching for the telephone when someone rapped on the door.

He put down the drink and opened it. There were two men in the dingy hallway. The nearer one crowded the door just enough to prevent its being closed again, and asked, "Your name John Ingram?"

"Yes," he said. "What is it?"

The other flipped open a folder containing a badge. "Police. We'd like to talk to you."

He frowned. "About what?"

"We'd better come inside."

"Sure." He stepped back. They came in and closed the door. One took a quick look into the bathroom, and then the clothes closet, reaching in to pat the suit hanging there. Ingram went over to the suitcase lying open on its stand at the foot of the bed, and started to reach inside. "Keep your hands out of there," the other man ordered.

He straightened. "What the hell? I just wanted to put on some pants."

"You'll get 'em. Just stand back."

The one who'd checked the bathroom and the closet came over and riffled expertly through the contents of the bag. "Okay," he said. Ingram took out a pair of gray slacks and started to put them on. The two detectives noticed the scars. One of them opened his mouth to say something, but looked again at the big man's face and closed it.

"Who are you?" Ingram asked. "And what is it you want?"

It was the one near the doorway who replied. "I'm Detective Sergeant Schmidt, Miami Police." He was a dark, compactly built man in his early thirties with an air of hard-bitten competence about him, neatly dressed in a lightweight suit and white shirt. He nodded to the other. "This is Arthur Quinn. You're from Puerto Rico—is that right?"

"More or less," Ingram replied.

"What do you mean, more or less? That's what the hotel register says."

"I lived in San Juan for the past three years."

"What line of work are you in?"

"I was in the boat-repair business down there. Another man and I had a boatyard and marine railway."

"Is that what you're doing now?"

"No. We had a bad fire. He was killed in it, and his widow wanted out, so we liquidated what was left."

"What are you doing in Miami?"

"Looking for a boat."

"To buy, you mean?"

"That's right," he replied. "What's this all about?"

Schmidt ignored the question. "You checked in here the first time fifteen days ago, but you've been gone for the past eight. Where've you been?"

"Nassau. Tampa. Key West."

"When were you in Key West?" Quinn asked. He was a slender, graying man with a narrow face and rather cold eyes. He looked more like the manager of a loan company than a cop, Ingram thought.

"Sunday," he said. "A week ago yesterday."

The two men exchanged a glance. "And you went down there to look at a boat?" Quinn asked.

Ingram nodded. "A schooner called the *Dragoon*. What about it?"

Quinn smiled. It didn't add any appreciable warmth to his face. "We thought you knew. The *Dragoon* was stolen."

Ingram had started to take a drink of the whisky. He lowered the glass, stared blankly at the two men, and went over and sat down beside the desk. "Are you kidding? How could anybody steal a seventy-foot schooner?"

"It seems to be easy, when you know how," Quinn replied. He moved nearer the desk. Schmidt leaned against the corner of the bathroom and lighted a cigarette.

"When did it happen?" Ingram asked.

"Oddly enough, the next night after you were aboard," Quinn said.

"And what is that supposed to mean?" Ingram asked quietly.

"It means you'd better come up with some answers. Somebody cased that job, and you look mighty good for it."

"You mean just because I was aboard? That boat was for sale, and open to inspection by anybody."

"The watchman says you were the only one that'd been aboard for nearly a month. He gave us a description of you, and we traced you back here."

"Description? Hell, I told him my name, and where I lived."

"He says you gave him some name, but he couldn't remember it. So it could have been a phony."

"Well, I'll have to admit that makes sense."

"Don't get snotty, Ingram. You can answer these questions here, or I can take you back down there and let you answer 'em. I'm from the Monroe County Sheriff's Department. That boat had been lying there at her mooring in the harbor for nearly a year, but whoever stole it knew she was still in condition to go to sea."

"Maybe they towed her away."

"She left under her own power." Quinn leaned his arms on the desk and stared coldly. "So how would they know there was even an engine aboard, let alone whether it'd run or not, or whether there was any fuel in the tanks, or the starting batteries were charged? You were on there all afternoon, poking into everything, according to old Tango. You started the engine and ran it, and inspected the rigging and steering gear, took the sails out of their bags and checked them—"

"Of course I did. I told you I was looking for a boat to buy. You think I went down there just to find out what color it was painted? And, incidentally, what was the watchman doing all the time they were getting away with it? He lived aboard."

"He was in the drunk tank of the Dade County jail. Clever, huh?"

"Dade County? How'd he get up here?"

"He was helped. He went ashore Monday night in Key West and had a few drinks, and all he can remember is he ran into a couple of good-time Charlies in some Duval Street bar. About three o'clock in the morning a patrol car found him passed out on the sidewalk on Flagler Street here in downtown Miami. He didn't have any money to pay a fine, so it was three days before he got out, and it took him another day to thumb his way back to Key West and find out the *Dragoon* was gone. Of course, everybody around the Key West water front knew it was, but didn't think anything of it. He'd already told several people there'd been a man aboard thinking of buying it, so they took it for granted it'd been moved to Marathon or Miami to go on the ways for survey. See? Just a nice convenient string of coincidences, so the boat was gone four days before anybody even realized it was stolen."

"I was in Tampa Monday night," Ingram said. "Also Tuesday, and Tuesday night."

"Can you prove it?"

"Sure. You can check with the Grayson Hotel there. Also with a Tampa yacht broker named Warren Crawford. I was in his office a couple of times, and aboard a ketch named the *Susannah*. If you'll look in the breast pocket of my coat you'll find the receipted hotel bill. And the stub of an airline ticket from Tampa to Nassau, Wednesday morning, and a receipted hotel bill from Nassau for Wednesday night to last night. Then there's a Pan American Airways ticket stub for the flight from Nassau back to Miami. I landed here at three-forty this afternoon and came straight to the hotel. Anything else?"

Schmidt had already removed the receipts and ticket stubs from the coat and was riffling through them. "Seems to be right."

"But he could still have cased the job," Quinn insisted. "The whole thing's too pat. And if he was just the finger man, he'd make sure he had an alibi." He whirled on Ingram. "Let's take another look at this pipe-dream you were going to buy, the *Dragoon*. What'd you expect to do with it?"

"Sail it out to Honolulu. I'm thinking of going back in the charter business. That's what I used to do, here and in Nassau."

"You know the owner's asking price?"

"Sure. Fifty-five thousand dollars."

The detective surveyed the room with a contemptuous smile. "You must be one of those eccentric millionaires."

Ingram felt his face redden. "What I pay for hotel rooms is my business."

"Come off it, Ingram! You expect us to believe a man living in a fleabag like this really intended to buy a fifty-five-thousand-dollar yacht? How much money have you got?"

"That's also my business."

"Suit yourself. You can tell us, or sweat it out in jail while we find out ourselves. What bank's your money in?"

"All right, all right. The Florida National."

"How much?"

"About twelve thousand."

"We can check that, you know. There'll be somebody at the bank till five."

Ingram gestured toward the telephone. "Go ahead."

"So you expected to buy a fifty-five-thousand-dollar yacht with twelve thousand?"

It might have been more sensible to explain, but he was growing a little tired of Quinn's attitude and he'd never been a man who took kindly to being pushed. He leaned forward in the chair and said, very softly, "And if I did? Quote me the law against it, by section and paragraph. And stop breathing in my face."

"Come on, Ingram! Let's have it. How many of you were there, and where's the boat headed?"

"If you won't take my word for it, call the owner. I wrote to her."

"In a pig's eye. You wouldn't even know who the owner is."

"Mrs. C. R. Osborne, of Houston, Texas. Her address is in that black notebook in my bag."

Schmidt gave him a thoughtful glance, and removed the notebook. Quinn, however, smiled coldly, and said, "Funny she didn't mention it. We talked to her about an hour ago and told her we were looking for a man named Ingram, but she'd never heard of you."

"You mean she's here in town?" he asked.

"Yes, she's here," Schmidt said. "She flew in this afternoon. When did you mail that letter?"

"Saturday morning, from Nassau," he replied. "Maybe she left Houston before it was delivered."

"We can find out. But what'd you say in it?"

"I made her an offer of forty-five thousand for the *Dragoon*, subject to the usual conditions of survey."

"And payable how?"

"Cash."

"All right," Schmidt said crisply, "if you *did* write a letter, which I doubt, it has to be a bona-fide offer, or a phony—in which case it's probably a deliberate alibi. You haven't got forty-five thousand dollars. So what were you going to use for money? Put up or shut up."

Ingram hesitated. Then he shrugged wearily, and said, "All right. I was acting for a third party."

"Who?"

"His name's Fredric Hollister, and he's president of Hollister-Dykes Laboratories, Inc., of Cleveland, Ohio. They manufacture ethical drugs. He's at the Eden Roc Hotel; go ahead and call him."

"Why didn't you tell us this in the first place?" Schmidt demanded.

"Partly, I suppose, because it was none of your damned business," he said. "But principally because he didn't want it known the buyer was a corporation until after the deal was set, because of the effect it might have on the price. I was to select the boat, subject to his final approval, and then take over as captain. We'd pretty well settled on the *Dragoon* after I gave him the report on it Sunday night, but decided to wait till I'd looked at the others in Tampa and Nassau before we committed ourselves. I'm supposed to call him this afternoon."

Schmidt nodded. "Can I use your phone?"

"Sure. Go ahead."

The detective picked it up. "Get me the Eden Roc Hotel, in Miami Beach," he said, and waited. The room was silent except for that faint humming of the air-conditioner. "Mr. Fredric Hollister, please . . . Oh? . . . Are you sure? . . . And when was this?"

Ingram stared at his face, conscious of a very cold feeling that was beginning to spread through his stomach.

14

Schmidt hung up, and snapped, "Get your clothes on, fella."

"What is it?"

"Hollister checked out of the Eden Roc a week ago. On Monday night."

2

His leg hurt. He'd smoked the two cigars he had, and the cigarettes they gave him tasted like hay. They sent out for coffee. Quinn and Schmidt questioned him, moving like cats around the table where he was seated, and then Schmidt was gone and there was another man, named Brenner. There was one window in the bleak interrogation room, covered with heavy screen, but from where he sat he could see nothing but the sky. He thought it was still raining. It didn't seem to matter. Quinn went out, and came back shepherding an old man with dirty white whiskers and sharp black eyes, an old man who clutched a comic book in one hand and a crumpled and strangely bottle-shaped paper bag in the other and pointed dramatically from the doorway like some ham in an amateur production of *Medea* or *King Lear,* and cackled, "That's him! That's him!" It was the watchman, the old shrimper who'd lived aboard the *Dragoon.*

"Hello, Tango," Ingram said wearily, to which Tango made no reply other than to heighten the fine theatrical aspect of this confrontation by leaning further into his point and belching. "Ain't nobody'd ever forget a big flat face like that," he announced triumphantly, and was gone, presumably back to the bottle. The identification seemed rather pointless, since he admitted being aboard the *Dragoon,* but maybe it was something technical about preparing the case.

Schmidt came back, and Brenner left. Schmidt leaned

15

on the other end of the table with an unlighted cigarette in his mouth, and said, "All right, let's try again. Who's Hollister?"

"All I know is what he told me," Ingram replied.

"We just heard from Cleveland. There is no such outfit as Hollister-Dykes Laboratories—if that's news to anybody. And he paid his hotel bill with a rubber check. How long have you known him?"

"I didn't know him at all. I met him just twice."

"How did you meet him?"

"I told you. He called me at the La Perla Hotel."

"When?"

"A week ago last Saturday. He said he had a proposition that might interest me, and asked if I'd come over to Miami Beach and see him."

"He just pulled your name out of a hat, is that it?"

"No. He said I'd been recommended to him by a couple of yacht brokers."

"He mention any names?"

"No. It didn't occur to me to ask, at the time. But there are any number of people around the Miami water front who could have told him about me. I've been in and out of here for years. Anyway, he seemed to know all about me, and wanted to know if I'd had any luck in finding a boat. I told him no."

"This was over the phone?"

"Yes."

"So you met him at the Eden Roc?"

"That's right. In his suite, about two p.m. Saturday. He explained who he was, and gave me a rundown on the deal he had in mind. The company wanted an auxiliary ketch or schooner, seventy feet or longer, one that would accommodate eight guests in addition to the crew. It would operate out of Miami, and be used for conferences and company entertainment, that sort of thing—deductible as a business expense, of course. I was to get five hundred and fifty a month as skipper, and during periods when nobody from the company was using it I could operate it as a charter boat on a commission basis. I wasn't crazy about the idea, because I'd rather work for myself, but I was in no position to be choosy. We didn't have the boat-

16

yard fully insured, and three-quarters of it belonged to Barney's widow, anyway, so by the time I'd settled my hospital and doctor bills I had less than thirteen thousand left. Any kind of boat I could use at all would run twenty-five thousand, and I just didn't have enough cash to talk to anybody. So I told him I'd take it.

"He had a list of five boats the company had been considering. The *Dragoon* in Key West, *Susannah* in Tampa, and three over in Nassau. He suggested I look at the *Dragoon* first, since it seemed to be the most promising. I went down to Key West Sunday morning, spent all afternoon on it, and flew back that night. I called Hollister, and he asked me to come on over and give him the report. I met him in his suite again, and we spent about two hours going over all the dope I had on it—sketches of the interior layout, inside dimensions, estimates on minor repairs, condition of the auxiliary engine, rigging, sails, and so on. The boat had been kept up, in spite of the fact it hadn't been used for a long time. He liked it. I told him that of course any offer we made would be subject to her passing survey. You don't buy a boat just on preliminary inspection. He suggested we hold off final decision until I'd looked at the others, but that if I still liked the *Dragoon* we'd get in touch with Mrs. Osborne and try forty-five thousand dollars. I left for Tampa Monday morning, and then went on from there to Nassau on Wednesday."

"He didn't say anything about calling him from Tampa with a report on the *Susannah?*"

Ingram's face hardened. "No. In fact, he said he'd probably be in West Palm Beach the next few days at a house party, and just to wait till I got back from Nassau."

Quinn came around in front of him and leaned on the table. "That's a great story. I love it. It covers you from every angle except being a chump, and there's no law against that."

"I can't help it. That's exactly the way it happened."

"Then you just swallowed all this whole?" Schmidt asked. "It never occurred to you to question it?"

"Why should it?" Ingram demanded. "His story made sense. Corporation-owned boats are nothing new. He had

17

all the props. He was living in a suite on the ocean side, with a sundeck. He gave me his card. It said he was Fredric Hollister, president of Hollister-Dykes Laboratories. When I was there the first day, he got a long-distance call from the home office in Cleveland—"

Schmidt gestured pityingly. "From some joker on a house phone in the lobby."

"Sure, I suppose it's an old gag, if you're looking for it. But why should I? And don't forget, he fooled the hotel too."

"I know," Schmidt said. "And to do that, he'd have to have more than a business card. He's beginning to smell like a real con artist to me. But that's the stupid part of it—what the hell would a con man want to steal a boat for?"

"You tell me," Ingram said. "He can't sell it. And he can't even leave the country in it without papers."

"Who paid your expenses while you were looking at all these boats?"

"Apparently I did. He gave me a check for two hundred dollars and said if they ran over that to keep a record and I'd be reimbursed. That's the reason I kept all those receipts."

"Where's the check?"

"I couldn't cash it before I left, because it was the week end, but I had enough cash of my own to carry me, so I mailed it in to the bank from Tampa. On Tuesday afternoon, I think." He tossed his checkbook over in front of Schmidt. "The deposit's entered on my stubs."

Schmidt looked at it, and nodded to Quinn. Quinn went out.

"Can you describe him?" Schmidt asked.

"He was in his late thirties, I'd say. Close to six feet. On the slim side, but big-boned and rangy and sunburned, with big hands. A tennis type. Blue eyes, as I recall. Butch-cut hair. I'm not sure, but I think it was sandy, maybe with a little gray in it. Lot of personality and drive —one of those guys with the bone-crushing grip and the big grin."

"You didn't notice what kind of watch he was wearing?"

"Yes, as a matter of fact, I did. It was an oversized thing

with a lot of gingerbread on it. Chronograph, I think they call it. You know, little windows with the day of the month and day of the week, and a sweep second hand."

Schmidt removed a watch from the pocket of his coat and set it on the table. "Like this?"

Ingram glanced at it in surprise. "Yes. That looks just like it. Same type of filigree gold case, and everything. Where'd you get it?"

Schmidt lighted the cigarette he had stuck in the side of his mouth. "It was picked up at sea."

Ingram stared. "How's that again?"

"Couple of men in a fishing boat brought it in. The *Dorado*—one of those fifty-thousand-dollar deals you use for marlin—"

"Sport fisherman."

"Yeah. Anyway, they were bringing this *Dorado* back to Miami from the Virgin Islands. And yesterday afternoon a little before sunset they sighted a rowboat—a dinghy, I think you call it. Nobody in it; just drifting around in the ocean by itself. They went over and picked it up. There was an outboard motor clamped on the back, and some man's clothes in the bottom—sneakers and a pair of dungarees and a shirt. The watch was in one of the pockets of the dungarees. They got into Miami early this morning and turned the whole thing over to the Coast Guard. The Coast Guard figured there might be a chance it was the *Dragoon*'s and called us. We went out and got a description, and called Mrs. Osborne to see if she could identify it. She wasn't sure—she's not too familiar with the *Dragoon*—but Quinn brought old Tango up from Key West, and he identified it."

"Where did they pick it up?" Ingram asked.

"South of here somewhere. The Coast Guard told me, but I'm no navigator."

Schmidt went out, leaving him in the custody of a uniformed patrolman who chewed a pencil stub and scowled at a crossword puzzle. When he returned, some ten minutes later, Quinn was with him.

"We're not going to hold you," Schmidt said curtly. "But before you go, we want you to look at some pictures."

19

Ingram sighed with relief. "Then you located my letter to Mrs. Osborne?"

"Yes. She called her maid at home. The letter apparently came this morning after she'd left for Miami. The maid read it to her, and it checks with what you told us. We also got hold of one of the officers working late at the bank, and he dug out that check Hollister gave you. It was the same phony account he stabbed the hotel with. It bounced, of course, but they hadn't got the notice out to you yet."

"Then you're convinced?"

"Let's put it this way—you helped steal that boat, but there's no proof you did it with intent. I don't know whether you were just a sucker, or smart enough to make yourself look like one, but either way we can't hold you."

"You die hard, don't you?"

"You learn to, in this business." Schmidt jerked his head. "Let's go see if you can pick Hollister out of some mug shots."

They went downstairs to another room that was harshly lighted and hot. The two detectives sat watching while he scanned hundreds of photographs—hopefully, and then with increasing anger as the hope faded—trying to find the man who'd called himself Hollister. He knew he was still suspect, and failure to turn up Hollister's picture would certainly do nothing to lessen their suspicion. There was anger at himself for having been taken in, and a burning desire to get his hands on the man who'd done it.

"I think this is a waste of time," Quinn said, after an hour.

"Haven't you got any more?" he asked.

"No. That'll do." There was curt dismissal in the tone. Ingram stood up. "Where is Mrs. Osborne staying?"

"I don't think I'd bother Mrs. Osborne, under the circumstances," Schmidt said. "That might have been the last fifty-thousand-dollar yacht she had."

"What about the *Dorado?* Do you know where she's tied up?"

"No. And what difference does it make?"

"I want to find out where they picked up that dinghy."

"Why?"

"Just say I'm curious. There's something damned funny about it."

"You were never more right," Quinn said coldly. "So why don't you just get out while you're ahead?"

When he emerged on the street the rain had stopped and it was dusk. Neon flamed hotly beneath the darkening blue bowl of the sky, and tires hissed on wet pavement in the ceaseless river of traffic. He walked back to the hotel, feeling his shirt stick to his back with perspiration. The desk clerk looked up with a nervous smile. "Uh—I hope everything's all right."

"Yes," he said.

"I hope you don't think—I mean, there wasn't anything I could do. They told me to call them if you checked back in—"

"It's all right. The key, please."

"Yes, *sir.*" The clerk whirled and snatched it from the pigeonhole. There was a slip of paper with it. "Oh. You had a phone call. It was about a half hour ago."

Ingram read the scribbled message. *Call Mrs. Osborne. Columbus Hotel.*

That was strange. But maybe she wanted to unburden herself of a few remarks on the subject of meat-heads who helped steal her boat. Probably an imperious old dowager with a voice like a Western Ocean bosun. Well, he intended to call her, but she could wait a few minutes; right now the important thing was to find the *Dorado* before her crew left for the night. The chances were that he was too late already. He strode to the telephone booth in the corner of the lobby, looked up the number of the Coast Guard base, and was just starting to dial when someone rapped on the glass panel of the door. It was the clerk.

He pushed it open. "Yes?"

"She's on the line now, sir. She just called back. You can take it on the house phone."

"Oh." He retrieved his dime and walked over to the desk. He might as well get it over with. The clerk patched him through on the small switchboard and disappeared into his room in back.

"Hello," he said. "Ingram speaking."

21

"This is Mrs. Osborne." The voice was rather husky, and sounded much younger than he'd expected. "Would you come over to the Columbus right away? There is something very important I'd like to discuss with you."

"What?" he asked.

"Just say that it has to do with the *Dragoon,* and that it's quite urgent. I think you could help me."

This appeared to make very little sense, but he realized asking questions would only waste more time. "All right," he said, "I'll be there as soon as I can make it. But first I want to try to get hold of the captain of the *Dorado*—"

"That won't be necessary," she broke in. "I've already talked to him."

"Did he tell you where they picked up the dinghy?"

"Yes. I have the whole story."

"I'm on my way. Where shall I meet you?"

"Just come up to my room."

It was less than ten minutes later when he stepped out of the elevator at the Columbus and strode down the carpeted and air-conditioned quietness of the corridor looking at the numbers. When he knocked, she answered almost immediately, and for a second he thought he must have the wrong room. Even hearing her voice over the telephone hadn't entirely prepared him for this.

Somehow, a woman who owned a seventy-foot yacht in her own name figured to be a graying and wealthy widow on the far side of fifty, at least, but this statuesque blonde with the flamboyant mop of hair couldn't be much over thirty. She wore a green knit dress that did her figure no harm at all, and he had a quick impression of a well-tended and slightly arrogant face with a bright red mouth, high cheekbones, sea-green eyes, and a good tan. "Come in, Captain," she said. "I'm Rae Osborne."

He stepped inside. The room was the sitting room of a suite, furnished with a pearl-gray sofa, two armchairs, and a coffee table. At the far end was a window with flamingo drapes. The door into the bedroom was on the left. There was soft light from the lamps at either end of the sofa. The thing that caught his eye, however, was the chart spread out on the coffee table. He stepped nearer, and saw it was the Coast & Geodetic Survey No. 1002, a general chart of the Florida Straits, Cuba, and the Bahamas. A highball glass stood in the center of it, in a spreading ring of moisture. He winced.

"Sit down," she said, with a careless gesture toward the armchair in front of the coffee table. She seated herself opposite it on the sofa and crossed her legs, the knit skirt hiking up over her knees and molding itself against the long and rather heavy thighs. He wondered if he was supposed to look appreciative. Then he decided he was being unfair; it was just that highball glass on the chart. She picked up the glass, rattled the ice in it, and took a drink, not bothering to offer him one. If this was the new look in yachting, he was caring less and less for it. You are in a nasty mood, he thought.

"You *are* a captain, aren't you?" she asked. "That's what they called you."

"I don't have a boat now," he said. "As you may have heard. But who called me?"

"Some people I talked to about you. Lieutenant Wilson of the Coast Guard, and a yacht broker named Leon Collins. They said it was stupid. You never stole anything in your life."

"Thanks," he said laconically.

She shrugged. "I'm just repeating what they said. But anyway, I'm willing to take their word for it. You didn't know that man Hollister, did you?"

"No," he said.

"Would you tell me what he looked like?"

He repeated the description he'd given the police. She listened intently, but with no change of expression. "I see."

"What did you want to see me about?" he asked.

"I want you to help me find the *Dragoon*."

He frowned. "Why me?"

"For several reasons. I'll get to that in a minute. But will you?"

"Believe me, there's nothing I'd like better than to find the *Dragoon*. And Hollister," he added grimly. "But if the police can't locate her——"

"She's at sea. Outside police jurisdiction."

"How do you know?"

23

"Oh, I forgot—you still don't know where the dinghy was picked up."

"No," he said.

"It was right here." She leaned over the chart and indicated a pencil mark with one red-lacquered fingernail. It was in the open sea, far out over the western edge of the Great Bahama Bank along the Santaren Channel, probably a hundred and fifty miles south-southeast of Miami. "At five-thirty yesterday afternoon."

"The time doesn't mean much," he said. "There's no telling how long ago they lost it, or where. They could be five hundred miles from there by now."

She shook her head. "Didn't they tell you about the clothes, and the watch?"

"Yes. But what about them?"

"The watch was still running."

"Oh," he said. Then the dinghy must have been adrift for less than twenty-four hours. "Are you sure of that?"

"Yes. I went down and talked to the captain of the *Dorado* myself. And the Coast Guard doesn't think the *Dragoon* was under way when they lost it."

"No, of course not, if they lost it out there. They wouldn't have been towing it. But, look—the men in the *Dorado* didn't see anything of the schooner at all?"

"No. They watched with binoculars until it got dark, but they didn't really search the area. She might have been in over the Bank somewhere. Maybe anchored."

"Not for long, unless they were gluttons for punishment," he said. "Except in a dead calm, it'd be like riding a roller-coaster. With fifty to seventy-five miles of open water to windward—"

"But it's all real shallow—or is shoal the word you use? Less than four fathoms, according to the chart."

"It can still kick up a nasty chop, in any breeze at all. Not to mention the surge running in from the Santaren Channel. It's more likely they were in trouble of some kind."

"Then she might be still there. Will you help me find her?"

"How?" he asked.

"How would I know?" she asked, rattling the ice in the

24

glass. "That's why I'm asking you. Maybe we could charter a boat?"

He shook his head. "You'd just be wasting money."

"Why?"

"I don't think you realize what you're up against. In the first place, that position you've got marked is where they *think* they were when they picked up the dinghy. Big-game fishing guides aren't the world's greatest navigators, as a rule. That far at sea, on dead reckoning, they could have been as much as twenty miles out. Add another thirty for the possible drift of the dinghy in the currents and tides along the edge of the Bank, and you're in real trouble. You have any idea of the area of a circle with a radius of fifty miles?"

"God no, you figure it out."

"Around eight thousand square miles. That's not somebody's front yard."

"But—"

"Furthermore, that Bank is nothing to fool with—especially at night or in poor light conditions. It's several thousand square miles of shoals, reefs, coral heads, and sand bars, and it's poorly charted, especially down there where you want to go. But disregarding all that for the moment, what good would it do if you get lucky and find her? Assuming, I mean, that the people who stole her are still aboard? There's no way you can regain possession or have 'em arrested until she goes into port somewhere; out on the open sea's a poor place to try to call a cop."

"Well, you're sure not much help, are you?" she asked. "Or maybe you just don't want the job? Can't you use the money?"

He stifled the slow burn of anger. "I'm trying to keep you from throwing yours away. I'm just as interested in finding the *Dragoon* as you are, but you'll never do it that way."

"Well, what about a plane?"

"You'd have a better chance of finding her, if she's still in that area. But you couldn't get aboard, if you did."

"At least I'd know where she is—and whether she's in trouble. What kind of plane would it take?"

"An expensive one."

"That doesn't matter. Where can we get one?"

"Why do you keep saying we?" he asked. "If you charter a plane, what do you need me for?"

"As I said, for several reasons. You're an experienced yachtsman. You've been sailing boats all your life. So you'd be able to tell if she was in trouble of some kind. But the main reason is I'm not sure I'd recognize the *Dragoon* if I saw her. They must have repainted her and changed the name."

He remembered then what Schmidt had said about her not being very familiar with the schooner. It also occurred to him that he knew nothing about her whatever except that presumably she was a widow; the ad in *Yachting* had listed the schooner under her own name. Alarm bells began to go off in his head. He glanced at her left hand. She wore engagement and wedding rings, but that didn't prove much.

"Why don't you think you'd recognize her?" he asked.

"I've been aboard her only once."

"How's that?"

"My husband took her in on some property he sold about a year ago, just before he died. Since the estate was settled, I've been trying to sell her. But to get back to the subject, you'd recognize her, wouldn't you?"

"I think so," he said.

"Good. Now, about the plane?"

"Not so fast. Maybe Hollister made me a little gun-shy, but this time I'd like some proof. How do I know you're Mrs. Osborne?"

"Well!" He thought for a moment she was going to tell him that *anybody* knew who Mrs. C. R. Osborne was, but she fooled him. "You're pretty hard-boiled, aren't you?"

"Not particularly," he said. "It's just that I've made my quota of bonehead plays for this week. But you don't have to bother digging up identification. Just tell me what I said in that letter."

She repeated it almost exactly as he had written it. "Are you satisfied now?"

"Yes." Then it occurred to him that his manners were almost as bad as hers. "And, incidentally, I want to thank you for going to all that trouble to call back to Houston to verify it."

She shrugged. "No trouble. Now what about the plane?"

"You're sure you want to go to all that expense, just to see if she's out there? She's insured, isn't she?"

She nodded. "Against marine risk, as I get the picture. But I don't think the policy covers theft, and if something happens to her out there and I've got no witnesses or actual proof of loss, it might be years before I could collect."

That was possible, he thought. But the feeling persisted that she wasn't telling the truth—or at least not all of it. Well, it was none of his business. He bent over the chart, studying the position she had marked and estimating the distances. "I think Nassau would be the best bet. It's a little nearer, and McAllister Air Service used to have some big twin-engine amphibians that should be able to do it. Want me to call them now?"

"Sure."

He reached for the telephone on one of the small end-tables. While the operator put through the call he sat frowning thoughtfully at the chart. What could they have been doing out there? He was connected then with the office at Windsor Field in Nassau. McAllister had left for the night, but one of the pilots was still around, a man named Avery. He said they were still flying the amphibians.

"What's their range?" he asked.

"It depends on the load. What do you want to carry?"

"Just a couple of passengers. Here's the deal. . . ." He explained briefly, and asked, "Do you have a chart handy, any general chart that takes in the area west of Andros?"

"Yes, sir. There's one right in front of me."

"Good. Take a look at the outer edge of the Bank, opposite Cay Sal. Got it? They picked up the dinghy at about 23.30 north, just off the hundred-fathom curve in the Santaren Channel. If we wanted to fly a search pattern around that point, how much of the area could we cover and still not have to walk home?"

"Hmmm . . . Just a minute . . . We could stay down there close to two hours and still get back all right."

27

"What's the rate?"

"A hundred and twenty-five dollars an hour."

"Just a minute." He placed a hand over the transmitter and relayed the figure to Mrs. Osborne.

She nodded. "Tell him we'll be there as soon as we can."

He spoke into the instrument. "Okay. I think there's a Pan American flight out of here early in the morning—"

"Yes. Flight 401. Arrives Nassau at nine a.m."

"Check. And if we can't get space on it, I'll cable you what flight we will be on. That okay?"

"Yes, sir. So unless we hear from you, we'll have her fueled and ready for nine a.m."

He broke the connection, got the hotel operator again, and asked for Pan American Airways. They were in luck; space was available on flight 401. He made the reservations and hung up.

"It's all set," he said. "I'll meet you at the Pan Am counter at the airport about three-quarters of an hour before flight time."

"Good. Now about your pay—"

"There's no charge," he said.

She frowned. "What?"

"I helped them steal the boat, didn't I? The least I can do is help you find it."

"You can't be serious."

He stood up to leave. "Whether or not I did it with intent, as the police call it, doesn't change the facts. I'm at least partly responsible for their getting away with it."

"Well, you're an odd one, I must say." She regarded him for the first time with something approaching interest. "How old are you?"

"Forty-three."

"You don't look it."

"Thanks," he said. She didn't bother to rise. He walked to the door, fighting the stiffness in his leg, but paused with his hand on the knob. "That dinghy—when they found it, were there any oars in it?"

"No," she said. "Just the motor."

"Was there any gasoline in it? Or did they look?"

28

She stared down at the glass in her hand. "They looked," she said. "It was empty."

He nodded. The silence lengthened. "See you in the morning," he said, and went out.

3

It was a long time before he got to sleep. On the evidence, the theft of the *Dragoon* was no hare-brained, spur-of-the-moment stunt; it had been carefully thought out by men who knew what they were doing. Then by the same token they must have known they couldn't enter any port in the western hemisphere without the necessary documentation —which they couldn't possibly steal. So what had they planned to do? Stay at sea, or put her into orbit?

And how had they lost the dinghy? The police seemed to accept this as merely a routine incident—they'd been towing it, it came adrift, so what? But it wasn't that simple. They wouldn't have been towing it at sea; and certainly not with the motor and somebody's clothes in it. It would have been aboard, lashed down on the deckhouse. So they had put it over the side for something. But for what? The watch and the clothes were easier to understand, at least up to a point. The man—whoever he was—had taken them off to go in the water for some reason. But what reason? You were stumped again.

And what about Mrs. Osborne—aside from the obvious things like the good looks and bad manners? Something didn't quite ring true. The theft would have been reported to her as soon as the police learned of it themselves—last Friday, at the latest. That was four days ago. But she apparently hadn't thought it necessary to come to Miami until this morning; and then presumably she'd grabbed the first available plane after the police called to tell her about the dinghy. Why? It wasn't to identify the dinghy.

She'd admitted over the phone she wasn't familiar enough with the *Dragoon*'s gear to be sure. And it wasn't necessary, anyway, because Tango identified it. So could it have been that watch that brought her flying in from Houston? Maybe she had an idea whose it was. But if so, why hadn't she told the police?

Forget it, he thought. All you have to do is find the schooner. He closed his eyes, and in back of them was the deadly flower of explosion. He had seen it nearly every night for the past two months, the same unvarying and frozen scene like a nightmare captured intact and imbedded in plastic. It was too late to stop him. Barney leaned forward to strike the torch. . . .

She was waiting near the Pan American counters when he arrived at the airport the next morning, and had already picked up the tickets and checked her bag. He tried to pay for his, but she brushed the money aside impatiently. "Don't be silly, I'll pay the expenses."

She was as attractive in the light of early morning as she had been under the softer illumination of the night, but her face showed signs of weariness, as though she hadn't slept well. She wore a crisp white linen skirt and short-sleeved blouse, and carried a heavy binocular case slung over her shoulder. When their flight was announced they went out and boarded the plane, and she slept all the way across to Nassau. They landed at Windsor Field at nine a.m. and filed through Immigration and Customs. He was gathering up their suitcases at the Customs counter when they were approached by a tall and sun-reddened man in tropical whites. "Captain Ingram?" he asked.

He nodded. "You're from McAllister?"

"Yes. I'm Robin Avery."

They shook hands, and he introduced Mrs. Osborne. Avery had a spiky red mustache and very cool blue eyes and spoke with a clipped economy of words that was suggestively British, though with no discernible accent. He motioned for a porter to collect the bags. "Leave those in the office until we get back, if you like," he said.

They followed him over to the office next to the McAllister hangar. Mrs. Osborne produced a sheaf of traveler's checks and made a deposit on the charter. Avery unrolled a chart on the counter and brought out a pair of parallel rulers. "Any particular preference as to a starting point?"

"Yes," Ingram said. "Why not hit the southern end of the area first?" He lined up the parallel rulers and walked them across the chart to the compass rose. "A course of two hundred True will put us over the hundred-fathom curve about forty miles south of where the dinghy was found. From there we could fly an east-west pattern out over the Channel and back in over the Bank with about ten-mile spacing."

"Right," Avery agreed. He rolled up the chart and they went out to where the big amphibian squatted on the apron in white sunlight. There were three seats on each side of the narrow aisle in the after compartment. "Who'd like the co-pilot's seat?" Avery asked, with a hopeful glance at Mrs. Osborne. "Visibility's much better up there."

She nodded to Ingram. "Your eyesight's probably better than mine at this sort of thing. I'd rather you took it."

"Okay." He followed Avery through the narrow doorway. They strapped themselves in. Avery started the engines, taxied out to the end of the runway, and called the tower for clearance. The engines roared, and they began to gather speed. Then they were airborne and climbing in a long turn toward Andros.

The blue chasm of the Tongue of the Ocean passed beneath them, and then the coral-toothed white surf of the barrier reef along Andros' eastern shore. The interior of the largest island of the Bahamas chain was a green mat of vegetation broken only by meandering creeks and great marshy lakes dotted with mangroves. The plane came out at last over the desolate west coast where the land shelved almost imperceptibly into the vast shallow seas of the Bahama Bank and the patterns of sand bars were like riffled dunes beneath the surface. Ahead and on both sides the horizon faded into illimitable distance, merging finally with the sky with no line of demarcation and seeming to move forward with their progress so that they remained always in the center. It was only by looking down at the

31

varying terrain of the bottom and the shifting patterns of color that it was possible to tell the plane was moving at all. The colors themselves were indescribable, Ingram thought; you had to see them to realize they could be that way, and he didn't believe that anybody ever entirely forgot them afterward. He wondered if Mrs. Osborne was enjoying them. He glanced aft, and she was leaning back in the seat with her eyes closed, smoking a cigarette. Well, maybe nobody'd ever told her it was an expensive ocean.

Andros faded away astern and they were alone above the immensity of the sea. Another thirty minutes went by. Then, a little over an hour after their take-off from Windsor Field, Avery said, "We should be coming up on the area now."

Ingram nodded. Ahead, just emerging from the haze of distance, was the long line sweeping across the horizon where the delicate shades of turquoise and powder blue and aqua changed abruptly to indigo as the western edge of the Bank plunged into the depths of the Santaren Channel. He stepped into the after compartment. Mrs. Osborne opened her eyes, and he pointed out the small window next to her seat.

She nodded, removed the binoculars from their case, and slung them about her neck. He bent down so as not to have to shout above the noise of the engines, and said, "I wouldn't try to use those too much. With this vibration, they'll pull your eyes out."

"All right," she said. She turned back to the window. Ingram returned to the co-pilot's seat. He unrolled the chart, penciled a mark on it where their course intersected the hundred-fathom curve, and set a clip-board in his lap. As they came over the drop-off, Avery banked in a gentle right turn, steadied up on the new course, and checked the time. "Two-seven-oh," he said. "Ten twenty-six."

"Right." Ingram wrote the figures on the pad attached to the clip-board without looking down as his eyes continued their search of the surrounding sea—ahead, starboard, out to the horizon, and below. The wind was out of the southeast with a light sea running, dotting the surface with random whitecaps that winked and were gone, but as far as the eye could see there was only emptiness. Fifteen minutes went by. They banked to the right and headed due north. Ingram noted the time and course. At the end of seven minutes they turned right again. "Ninety degrees," Avery called out as they steadied up. They were now flying back parallel to their first course and approximately ten miles north of it. Between changes of course, no one spoke. Avery flew mechanically while he searched the sector to port along with Mrs. Osborne. They came in over the Bank, turned north again, and then west once more. There was no sign of life, no craft of any kind, anywhere in the emptiness below them.

An hour dragged by. An hour and a half. They came up to and passed the area where the dinghy had been found. His leg began to bother him, and his eyes ached from staring. Once they sighted a small dot far to the westward and changed course with sudden hope. It was a commercial fishing boat over the Cay Sal Bank on the opposite side of the Channel. They picked up the pattern again, and went on, twenty-five miles west, ten miles north, twenty-five east, and then north again, squinting against the sunlit water below them and straining to pierce the haze of distance far out on the horizon. At 12:15 p.m., Avery made a last check of the fuel gauges, and said, "That's it for now." They flew back to Nassau and re-fueled.

They took off again, made the long run down across Andros and the Bank once more, and were back in the search pattern shortly after three. It was almost hopeless now, Ingram thought. They were already north of where the dinghy had been picked up, and working farther away from the area all the time. They went on, not speaking, eyes glued to the emptiness below and on all sides of them.

At 4:35 p.m. they were on an eastward leg. As they came in over the edge of the Bank, Avery checked the time and the remaining fuel, and said, "Best make the next leg a short one. Only about thirty minutes before we have to start back."

Ingram nodded. They started to turn to the left, while his eyes searched the blurred distance in over the Bank. "Hold it!" he called out suddenly. "I think I see something."

33

It was only an indistinct speck, far ahead and below them. He pointed. Avery saw it, and nodded. They continued on course, heading straight toward it. In another ninety seconds he could make out that there were two separate objects. One was a narrow rock or sand spit showing just above the surface; the other, however, was a boat and he felt a tingle of excitement along his nerves. He started to call out to Mrs. Osborne, and then was aware she had come forward and was crouched behind him peering over his shoulder. Avery changed course slightly to put the boat on the starboard side, and nosed down to lose altitude. He could see the masts now. There were two of them, the taller aft. The boat was a schooner, and a large one. He saw the large cockpit aft, the long, low deckhouses, the rakish bowsprit.

"There she is," he said. It was the *Dragoon*.

She was lying dead in the water, listing slightly to port with her sails furled. They went over at a thousand feet still losing altitude. Avery banked right to swing back. Ingram stared down to keep her in view, conscious of Mrs. Osborne's face touching his and her hand digging into his shoulder. She was clutching the binoculars in her other hand, trying to bring them to bear on the schooner's deck. He slid out of the seat, pushed her into it, and stood behind her. The schooner was momentarily lost to view then as Avery lengthened the radius of his turn. When they straightened out at last they were some four hundred feet above the water and about a mile astern. They flew up past her, less than a hundred yards off her port side, and he could see everything quite clearly.

Her hull was painted a light blue now, instead of white and while he couldn't make out the name lettered on her stern it was shorter than *Dragoon*. She lay roughly on a northerly heading about three hundred yards southwest of the dry sand bar, which was itself approximately that long, very narrow, and not over two or three feet above water at its highest point. The water was very shoal on all sides of the bar except for one twisting channel of slightly darker blue extending along its western side, past the *Dragoon*'s stern, and then on westward toward the outer edge of the Bank. The tide was flooding onto the Bank, flowing around her hull, but she lay broadside to it and unmoving. The deck was empty of any sign of life. Then they were past her, and Avery was climbing to gain altitude for another turn.

Mrs. Osborne had put down the binoculars and had her face pressed against the window, trying to see aft. "Are you sure it's the *Dragoon?*" she asked.

"Yes," he said. "There's no doubt of it."

"There's something funny about the way she's lying. What is it?"

"She's aground."

"I didn't see anybody. Did you?"

"No. I think she's been abandoned."

"There *must* be somebody. . . . What could have happened?"

"I don't know," he said.

Avery completed the turn and they came back, still lower and off the schooner's starboard side this time. She was in no immediate danger, Ingram thought, as long as the wind held out of the southeast. There was a short, choppy sea running across the Bank, but she was completely protected in the lee of the shoal surrounding the sand spit. A norther would break her up, but there was little chance of one in June. As they went past he swept the deserted deck with a cool professional eye. There appeared to be no damage. The sticks and rigging were all right as far as he could tell. The sails were sloppily furled, as though they had been stowed in the dark by farmers, but the booms were inboard, the main resting on its gallows. There was only one thing that appeared to be amiss, and that was hard to judge with the list she had. She could be a little low in the water. Maybe she had been holed on a reef somewhere and they'd deliberately beached her. But there was no anchor out, which would seem to indicate she'd been abandoned before she went aground. It was baffling.

Then they were past, and climbing. Ingram made an estimate of the position and marked it on the chart. Avery checked the time, and cautioned, "Can't cut it too fine. We'd best start for home."

"Could we go by just once more?" Mrs. Osborne asked.

Avery nodded. They made the turn and came back, higher this time. She stared down at the empty deck. Then the schooner was falling away behind them, looking helpless and forsaken in the lonely distances of the sea. When she disappeared at last, Mrs. Osborne turned away from the window. "How do we get aboard?"

"Charter a boat," Ingram replied.

"How long will it take?"

"Two days, at least. Maybe three."

"That's too long. Why don't we land out there with the plane?"

He glanced at Avery. The latter nodded. "Could be done, if there's not too much sea running. Early in the morning would be the best time. But you'd have to take it up with McAllister."

He started to point out that merely getting aboard wouldn't solve anything; the chances were they were going to need the help of another boat, and one with plenty of power, to pull her off. Then he reconsidered; there were several things in favor of it. He could size up the situation at first hand, see just what it was going to take to get her afloat again, and find out if there was any damage below the water line. Also, she might not be fast aground at all; she might merely have lodged there on a change of tide and float off herself on the next flood. With no anchor out, there was no telling where she would wind up. An abandoned boat was always in danger.

"What about getting over to her?" he asked.

"We have some rubber life rafts," Avery replied.

They landed in Nassau shortly before six. McAllister was still in the office. He was a portly Irishman with curly black hair, a cigar, and the affable charm of a successful politician. Ingram unrolled the chart on his desk and explained the situation.

"You're sure that's the position?" McAllister asked. "The chart doesn't show a sand bar there."

"I know," he said. "It doesn't mean anything. A lot of the Bank's pretty sketchy in the survey department, and those shoals and bars change with every storm. We checked the course on the way in, and wouldn't have any trouble finding it again."

"Any rocks or coral heads close to the surface?"

Avery shook his head. "No. There's plenty of water to he westward of the sand spit. Early in the morning, before he breeze gets up, we could bring her in well off the shoal nd taxi up in the lee of it while they go aboard."

"Okay," McAllister replied. "If it looks safe to you. What time do you want to take off?"

"The earlier the better. As soon as it's light."

"All right. We'll put one of those surplus life rafts board and have her ready."

Ingram retrieved their suitcases and they went around n front of the terminal and took a taxi downtown. As hey pulled away from the loading zone, she asked, 'What do you think happened? What became of them?"

"I don't know," he said.

"You don't think there's a chance anyone is still board?"

"No. They'd have made some attempt to get her off. There would have been a kedge anchor out astern, or ome roily water downstream if they'd been turning the ngine. She was apparently abandoned even before she drifted in there."

"But how? And why?"

He shook his head. "I wouldn't even try to guess. There's been no bad weather, and I didn't see any sign of damage. Hollister couldn't have taken her down there lone. There had to be others. And as far as we know, hey didn't even have another dinghy to get off with even f they'd wanted to. It makes no sense at all."

"But what about Hollister?"

"There's a good chance he's dead."

It was a moment before she answered. "Why?"

"He took off his clothes and that watch to go in the vater after something. He didn't come back into the linghy. And if he's not aboard the *Dragoon*, that doesn't eave much."

"I see," she said. He turned and glanced at her, but she vas staring out the window on the opposite side. She was ilent during the rest of the ride into town; when he sug-,ested the Pilot House Club as a good place to stay, she

37

merely nodded. When they came into the central busines
district she asked the driver to stop, and got out.

"I want to do some shopping," she said to Ingram
"Take my suitcase and the binoculars, and reserve a roor
for me. I'll be along later."

After he'd shaved and showered he ate a solitary dinne
in the patio near the pool. He didn't see her anywhere. H
crossed the road to the Yacht Haven; none of the skipper
he knew were around, so he walked downtown, driven b
restlessness, and had several bottles of beer in the Carlto
House bar. You're getting old, he told himself; you'v
been too many places for too many forgotten reasons, an
now you're going around again. Remembering the sam
place offset in different layers of time makes it too eas
to count the years in between and wonder where the
went. You wake up in the morning and they're speakin
Spanish outside your window, so it could be Mexico agair
and you remember lightering bananas down the Grijalv
River in a wheezy gasoline-powered tug with a string o
cranky barges and the goofy invincibility of youth, an
the salvage job off the Pánuco River bar below Tampic
when the tanker piled up on the south jetty because th
skipper wouldn't wait for a pilot and didn't know abou
the bad southerly set across the entrance during a norther
and then you realize the two memories are eleven year
apart and somehow they've shoved a whole war, severa
other countries, and a good deal of the western Pacifi
in between. And Nassau . . .

That had been the good time. Seven years of it, wit
Frances and the *Canción*. He'd met Frances in 1948 whe
she'd been one of a party of five Miami schoolteacher
who'd chartered the *Canción* for a week's trip to Eleu
thera. They were married that same year, and lived aboar
the ketch as skipper and mate in a very special and pri
vate world of their own happiness while carrying charter
along the New England coast in summer and around th
Bahamas in winter—until 1955. She'd flown home t
Seattle to visit her mother, and was going to drive back t
Chicago with friends to take the plane down to Miam
Everything had seemed to run down and stop then, o
that endless bright November afternoon in the Berr

38

slands with the wind blowing blue and clean from the north, when he got the word by radio. She'd been killed in an automobile accident at a place called Manhattan, Montana. While he stood there holding the handset of the radiotelephone in his hand waiting for the numbness to wear off and the thing to begin to get to him wherever it was going to start, it seemed the only thing he could think of was that if he could only isolate it and pin it down there must be a question in here somewhere for the boys who could always explain everything. After all the places he'd been in the world, the only thing he'd ever been handed that he wasn't sure he was going to be able to handle had happened to him in a place he'd never even heard of.

You've had too much beer, he thought, or you think too much when you drink. He left the bar and walked back, and it was after eleven when he came into the lobby of the Pilot House. The girl at the desk said Mrs. Osborne had tried to call him several times in the past hour. "Thank you," he said. He went on up to his room, looked at the telephone, and shrugged. The hell with Mrs. Osborne; he was going to bed. While he was unbuttoning his shirt, the telephone rang. He ignored it until the third ring, when it occurred to him the girl would have told her he was in now. He picked it up.

"I want to talk to you," she said. Her voice sounded blurred, and the words tended to run together.

"I was just going to bed."

"At eleven o'clock? Do you get a merit badge or something?"

"Can't it wait till morning?"

"No. Come over to my room. Or I'll come over there."

Stoned, he thought. He'd better humor her, or she'd be banging on the door. "All right." He put the instrument back on the cradle and went down the hall.

4

The door was ajar. When he knocked, she called out, "Come on in." He stepped inside. She had on a blue dressing gown and was sitting on the studio couch with her stockinged feet stretched out on the coffee table in front of it. Beside her feet there were a bottle of Bacardi about two-thirds full, two or three opened bottles of Coca-Cola, a pitcher of ice, and a paperback mystery novel. She had a glass in her hand.

She regarded him solemnly, and sniffed. "It's all right to close the door. You can always scream."

He was aware for the first time that she had a definite southern accent. Perhaps he'd heard it before but it just hadn't registered; he was a Texan too, and, although he'd been away so long that he'd lost all trace of it himself, he didn't always notice it in others when he heard it. She didn't appear to be outstandingly drunk, aside from the solemnity. The flamboyant mop of tawny hair was all in place, and her mouth nicely made up. But you never knew. There might possibly be other things in the world more unpredictable than a woman with too much to drink, but he'd never run into any of them. He wondered, without caring particularly, if she hit it this hard all the time. It'd be a shame. She was still a fine figure of a woman, but she must be between thirty and thirty-five, and at that age they didn't stay in there long against the sauce without being marked.

"You don't have to look so smug," she said. "I'm perfectly aware of it."

"What?"

"That my feet are on the coffee table."

"Los pies de la Señora Osborne están en la mesa," he said, with a parrot-like intonation.

40

She frowned. "What's that mean?"

"The feet of Mrs. Osborne are on the table. I don't now—it just sounded like one of those phrase-book eals. Would it be all right if we talked about your feet the morning?"

"Captain, I have a feeling that you don't entirely ap-rove of me. Do you?"

"I hadn't given it any thought," he said. "Does it mat-er?"

"Of course it matters. Don't you realize I might slash ly wrists?"

He said nothing, wondering if two adults could get into more asinine conversation. She probably wasn't drunk nough to throw things, so maybe after she got a little of out of her system, whatever it was, he could leave with-ut starting a scene that would bring down the hotel. 'here seemed no point in even trying to guess what had rought it on. It was possible, of course, that he'd muffed 1e cue back there when she'd asked him to register for 1em, though that was pretty farfetched; if she'd wanted to 1dulge in a little away-from-home affair, she was certainly ttractive enough to do better. There were plenty of ounger and more personable men available in a place like Jassau. It was more probable, if that were the case, that he'd merely expected him to make the bid so she could 1rn it down. In any event, it hadn't even occurred to him, o maybe he *was* getting old. Or, as she charged, he just idn't like her. Well, he didn't, particularly. Maybe that as the answer; she'd sensed it, and resented it—though e couldn't imagine why. With those green eyes and that igh-cheekboned and suggestively arrogant face she didn't trike you as somebody who normally bled a great deal ver the opinions of the rabble.

She was apparently lost in thought; maybe she'd forgot-en he was there.

"What did you want to see me about?" he asked.

She poured some more rum in the glass. "Hollister."

His eyes narrowed thoughfully. "What about him?"

"I wanted to ask you something. When he was giving ou this snow job, did he ever say anything about being doctor?"

41

"No."

"You're sure?"

"Positive."

"Just this moonshine about being president of a drug firm? Well, it *is* in the pattern, at that."

He began to have the feeling now that she wasn't as drunk as she appeared. She was faking it. "What are you talking about?"

"Still that same old medical angle," she mused, as if speaking to herself. "His mother must have been frightened by a pregnancy test."

"You know him, don't you?"

"Who says I do?"

"You spent over a thousand dollars today just to fly over the *Dragoon* with a pair of binoculars, looking for him."

"Maybe I was trying to find out."

"Who do you think he was?"

"It's nothing to you."

"No, but it might be to the police. Or had you thought of that?"

"Never mind the police. If I have to go out and recover my own boat, they can look after themselves. I tell you I don't know, anyway. I'm just guessing."

"Did he have a watch like that?"

"Yes," she said. "But that's no real proof. They're not too common, but still there are others."

"What about the description I gave you?"

"It could fit him. Along with a lot of other men. There's another thing, though, that's more important. You must have wondered why he wanted somebody else to survey the boat instead of going himself."

"Sure."

"He couldn't have gone himself because Tango would know him. He'd been aboard the *Dragoon* before."

He nodded. "That would make sense. But what would he want to steal it for?"

"I have no idea."

"Who was he?"

"He's just a man I used to know. His name's Patrick Ives. That is, if all these guesses are right."

"Did he know anything about sailing?"

42

"A little, I think. I know he's sailed small boats."

"Do you think he could have handled the *Dragoon*—with help, I mean? She's a little out of the plaything class."

"That I couldn't judge; I don't know enough about it myself. He did know navigation, though; he was a B-17 navigator during the Second World War."

"He was just asking for trouble if he didn't know how to handle a boat that size."

"Well, he seems to have found it, judging from where the *Dragoon* is now. Do you really think he's dead?"

Ingram nodded. "Naturally, there's no way to be sure, but I think he drowned."

She looked down at her glass. "I suppose so."

"Was he a doctor?" he asked.

"No," she said, without looking up. "He was a phony. He liked to pass himself off as a doctor when he was cashing rubber checks."

He nodded. "That sounds like him. I've got one of his checks."

"Well, it's no collector's item."

"You don't have any idea at all why he would steal the boat?"

"None whatever, as I told you once before. Would you like me to have that statement notarized, Captain?"

Well, Ingram reflected, he *could* tell her to take her schooner and go to hell—there was always the easy way out, if you wanted to quit. But it would be an admission of defeat in just as real a sense as any other failure to finish the job. And there was no use getting hacked at a drunk; that was stupid. If she *is* drunk, he thought. He'd given up trying to guess that one.

He went back to his room and lay staring up at the dark for a long time before he went to sleep. The whole thing was murkier than ever. Assuming she was correct, and Hollister's real name was Patrick Ives, you still didn't know anything. Why was she so concerned with catching up with him, and whether he was dead or not? And why in God's name would a con man and rubber-check artist want to steal a schooner which was of utterly no value to him and which he probably couldn't even sail in the first place?

That was about as sensible as trying to carry off a paved street.

He awoke drenched with sweat and tangled in the sheet, with the feeling that he had cried out in his sleep. When he turned on the light and looked at his watch, it was a little after two. Well, he wasn't dreaming about it as often now, and eventually the picture would fade; it wasn't as if there were any feeling of guilt, as though he'd panicked and left Barney there to flame like a demented and screaming torch. He'd got him out and over the side of the shattered boat with his own clothes aflame and Barney's flesh coming off on his gloves. It was too late, and Barney was already dead, but nobody could have saved him. It wasn't that. It was horror. It was the fear afterward, and wondering if he would ever be able to smell gasoline in a boat again without being sick with it.

It wasn't a very big boat that had killed Barney and burned the yard down back to the office and the gate. Her name was *Nickels 'n' Dimes,* and she was a beat-up old thirty-foot auxiliary sloop in for a number of minor jobs, including some engine overhaul and the installation of a new radiotelephone and a better ground plate on the outside of her hull. They had put on the copper strip when she was on the ways, and the bolt through the hull for the radio connection. She went back in the water Friday afternoon. The separate ingredients for disaster were a long week end, a slow leak somewhere in her fuel system, poor ventilation, and the fact that Barney—who had a poor nose anyway—had a cold on Monday morning. The catalyst was a torch. Barney had the radio ground cable connected to the through-bolt and was preparing to silver-solder it when Ingram came down the hatch and smelled the gas. He yelled, and at the same instant Barney struck the torch.

He'd left a call for four a.m. When the telephone rang, he was instantly awake. Opening the french windows, he stepped out onto the balcony facing the harbor channel and Hog Island. They were in luck; it was dead calm. The fronds of the coconut palms along Bay Street were motionless in the pre-dawn darkness that was beginning to show a faint wash of rose in the east. He called Mrs. Osborne,

44

found she was already awake, and hurriedly dressed in khaki trousers, T-shirt, and sneakers. When he came out into the corridor, she was just emerging from her room. She was wearing white calypso pants and sandals and a blue pullover thing with short sleeves. Her legs were bare. She looked very cool and fresh and attractive, and if she had a hangover there was no visible trace of it. Must have a constitution like a horse, he thought. He took her suitcase and went out to signal one of the taxis across the street while she settled the bill. She was silent on the ride to the airport. There was no apology, or even any reference to her behavior of last night. Maybe she didn't even remember it, he thought—not that it mattered. The airport restaurant was closed, but Avery had some coffee in the McAllister office. They drank a cup.

"We'll just leave your bag here," Ingram said. "I'll take mine, since I'll probably stay aboard. Even if we find we're going to have to charter a tug to get her off, we can't leave her abandoned out there."

They went out and boarded the plane. The deflated life raft was bundled up in back of the seats in the after compartment. Ingram motioned for her to take the co-pilot's seat, and strapped himself into one of those in back. Faint light was just breaking when they roared down the runway and took off. He lighted a cigar and settled back to wait. It would take over an hour.

Andros was a brooding dark mass below them, and then they were out over the vast distances of the Bank where the water lay hushed and flat in the pearly luminescence of dawn. The sun, peering over the curvature of the earth behind them, sprayed the underside of the wing with crimson and gold in momentary brilliance until Avery nosed down again and it was lost. After what seemed like hours, Ingram looked at his watch again. They should sight her in a few more minutes. He stepped through the narrow doorway and stood in back of Mrs. Osborne. She was staring out ahead. Two or three minutes later he tapped her lightly on the shoulder and pointed. "There she is." She nodded, but made no reply.

The distant speck grew and divided into its separate components of sand bar and boat. Avery began his de-

45

scent. Ingram spoke alongside his ear. "Let's take another look at her before we go in. Get an idea of the tide."

Avery nodded. The schooner was off to starboard and a thousand feet below as they went past. Ingram stared down at her. The empty deck still listed slightly to port in the early morning light, and there was about her something of the tragic helplessness of a beached and dying whale as she lay exactly as she had yesterday afternoon, on the same northerly heading. Avery swung in a wide circle and they came down past her only a few hundred feet above the water. Apparently nothing had changed at all except that the list might be slightly less, indicating the tide was higher. He studied the water moving ever so slowly past the imprisoned hull.

"Still flooding a little," he said above the roar of the engines. "But probably pretty close to slack high water right now. You won't drift much."

Avery nodded. "You want to go by again?"

"No. Let's put her down."

"Righto. Cinch up your belts."

Ingram went back and strapped himself in. He watched out the window as Avery swung west, toward the edge of the bank, made a preliminary run to study the water for possible obstructions, turned, and came in for the landing. Water, smooth as oil, came up toward them, and then they touched and the plane was drowned in a seething white curtain of spray. They slowed, and began to settle in the water. He unfastened his belt and went forward. They were about two miles west of the sand spit and the schooner. Avery turned. They began to taxi up toward her.

"We'd best not try to get too close," he said. "I don't trust those shoals around there."

"Within a half mile will do," Ingram replied. "And as long as the tide keeps flooding, you'd better go back to westward to wait for us."

"How long do you think you'll be aboard?"

"I can probably bring Mrs. Osborne back in a half hour or less. But suppose I call you on the radiotelephone, if it's still working? Have you got either of the intership channels?"

Avery nodded. "Call on 2638."

"Right," Ingram said. He stepped into the after compartment, attached the inflating bottle to the valve of the raft, and put enough air into it to keep it afloat. Avery came aft. He opened the door and they pushed the raft out. Ingram knelt in the opening and completed the inflation. Mrs. Osborne was standing behind them now. The plane rocked gently with little gurgling sounds under its hull as they swung around on the tide. Avery held the raft while Ingram helped her in. She settled herself aft. Ingram put his suitcase in, along with the air bottle and the light aluminum oars, and stepped down himself and pushed away from the plane.

He slid the handles of the oars through the tabs that served as oarlocks and began rowing. As soon as they were out from behind the plane, he looked over his shoulder and saw that Avery had approached nearer than he had expected; the *Dragoon* was not more than four hundred yards away. The sun was just coming up out of the sea beyond her, throwing her into silhouette. Beautiful, he thought—if she weren't so obviously aground. Boats in trouble always left you with an uncomfortable feeling.

It was still dead calm, and the water lay as flat as steel except for an occasional and almost imperceptible lift and fall from some vestigial remnant of surge running in from the Santaren Channel, attenuated by five miles of shoal water between here and the edge of the Bank. He dug in the oars. As soon as they were clear of the plane, Avery started the starboard engine, swung, and taxied toward the deeper water to the west. Ingram studied the water around and under them as he rowed. Judging from the color and from what he could see of the bottom straight down, it was sand and at least two fathoms deep all the way up to where the *Dragoon* was lying, and the channel was a good hundred yards wide. The schooner drew seven feet; if they could get her off into it, she could probably make it back to deep water without trouble, provided they made the attempt in good light.

But—he shot another glance over his shoulder—getting her off didn't look too promising as they came nearer.

47

The blue water of the channel was half a ship's length away from her stern. The deepest part of her keel would be still another thirty feet forward of that, so she might have to move back some sixty or seventy feet before she found enough water to float her unless the tide came a lot higher than it was now, and he was afraid it was very near to slack high at the moment.

The sound of the plane's engine died abruptly as Avery cut it off and let the plane come to rest about a mile away. They were now less than fifty yards from the port side of the schooner. He changed course to come around under her stern.

"Can't we go aboard on this side?" Mrs. Osborne asked.

"There's something I want to see first," he replied.

"Oh," she said. "The name."

Not exactly, he thought, but made no reply. She was leaning to the right, trying to get a glimpse of it. *"Lorna,"* she called out suddenly. "And look—you can still see a little of the old lettering under that blue paint."

He glanced around as they came in under the counter. She was right. The new name had been lettered in black over the light blue with which they'd painted the topsides, but at either end the *D* and the *n* of *Dragoon* still showed. It was a sloppy job of painting. He shipped the oars and caught hold of the rudder post; they stopped, and hung, suspended in utter silence. The tide was almost at a standstill. He waited for the ripples to die away, and then leaned over, peering straight down through water as transparent as gin. His eyes narrowed.

"What is it?" she asked.

"Look," he replied. "See that long gouge the keel made, leading backward toward the channel?"

"Yes. What does that mean?"

"She didn't drift in here. She was under way when she hit."

She looked up. "Then they were still aboard."

"Somebody was."

He noted that unconsciously they had lowered their voices. Well, there *was* something ghostly about it. Maybe it was the silence.

48

Why hadn't they at least tried to kedge her off? From the looks of the bottom they'd backed the engine down, throwing sand forward, but there was no sign of an anchor cable, even a broken one. It was possible, of course, that the dinghy was already gone, but they could have floated the anchor astern, using one of the booms for a raft, or carried it across the bottom a few steps at a time by diving. He'd better keep Mrs. Osborne on deck until he'd had a look below; there could be a body, or bodies.

He shoved away from the rudder post and took up the oars again. They went slowly up the starboard side. She was low in the water, all right. Several inches. This was the high side, the way she was listing, and the line of the old boot-topping was almost in the water. If you had her up to her proper water line, she'd be within a foot of floating right now. She must be holed. He peered down but couldn't see past the turn of the bilge. They continued forward, passed under the bowsprit, and came aft along the port side.

When they came abreast of the main he shipped the oars again and reached up to catch the shrouds just above the chainplates. With the port list, the deck was not too high above them. Gathering up the painter, he climbed on deck. He made the painter fast and reached down a hand for her. She scrambled up, ducked under the lifeline, and stood beside him.

The deckhouses were long and low, rising not over two feet above the deck, with small portholes along their sides. Two or three of the portholes were open, but he could see nothing beyond them because of the dimness inside the cabins. The sun was above the horizon now and warm on the side of his face as it gilded the masts and rigging. Everything was wet with dew. He stood for a moment looking along the sloping, deserted deck. There was an air of desolation about it as though the schooner had been abandoned for weeks, but he realized it was probably nothing more than a general untidiness that offended his seaman's sense of order. The sails were gathered in sloppy and dribbling bundles along the booms rather than properly furled, and at the bases of the fore- and mainmasts the falls of halyards and topping lifts lay helter-skelter in a confused jumble of rope. Neither of them had said a word. It was almost as though they were reluctant to break the hush.

They walked back to the break of the after deckhouse, and stepped down into the cockpit. It was a long one, and fairly wide, and at the after end of it were the binnacle, wheel, and the controls for the auxiliary engine. Ingram turned and looked back at the tracks they had left in the dew collected in millions of tiny droplets over the decks. There were no others.

"I'll have a look below," he said. "You wait here a minute."

"All right," she replied.

The companion hatch was open. He went down the ladder. After the sunlight on deck, the interior of the large after cabin was somewhat dim, but as his eyes came below the level of the hatch he saw several things almost at once. What appeared to be scores of long wooden cases were piled high on both sides of the cabin and in two of the four bunks, held in place by a criss-cross network of rope lashings. But it was one of the other bunks, the one on the port side forward, that riveted his attention and caused him to mutter a startled oath as he hurried down the last two steps. In it was the body of a slender, dark-haired man in khaki trousers, lying face down with one arm dangling over the side. He crossed to the bunk with three long strides and reached down to touch his arm, expecting to find it rigid. It was warm, and yielded to his hand, and in the brief fraction of a second in which this registered in his mind and the man began to turn on his side he heard Mrs. Osborne scream, *Look out!* and he turned himself. In back of him, leaning against the companion ladder behind which he'd apparently been hiding, was a hairy and half-naked giant cradling a Browning Automatic Rifle in the crook of his arm. He looked like a wartime atrocity poster.

"Welcome aboard, Herman," he said. "We're glad to see you."

5

The immobility of shock was gone then. "Get off!" Ingram shouted. He could see nothing of Mrs. Osborne except one slender hand grasping the top of the ladder railing, but knew she was looking down right on top of the man. The latter swung the muzzle of the BAR up through the hatch, and said, "Come on down, baby. That plane's a mile away. He can't hear you."

Ingram was already pushing off the bunk to lunge at him when he realized what he was doing and caught himself. Crashing into him with that BAR pointed up at her could cut her in two. At the same moment something pressed into his back just below his shoulder blades, and the man behind him said, "Relax."

Rae Osborne came down the ladder. The big man jerked his head toward the other bunk, opposite Ingram. "Sit down," he ordered. "You too, Herman."

Ingram stepped across and sat down beside her, silently cursing himself for an idiot. But how could he have known? There'd been no footprints in the dew up there. Apparently the big man guessed his thoughts, for he grinned. "We had a hunch you might be back early if you came by plane, so we stayed off the deck."

"All right, all right! What do you want?"

"Just a little help." He turned to Rae Osborne. "You'd be the owner, right?"

"I was under that impression," she said.

"And you brought Herman out here to see about getting this scow off the mud?"

"What business is it of yours?"

"Just checking, baby. I think we can use him."

She stared at him. "What are you talking about?"

"Experts. We're fresh out." He cradled the BAR in

one mammoth arm, and reached over to the shelf on the port bulkhead where the radiotelephone was installed. He switched on the receiver. He picked up a pack of cigarettes and shook one out, popped a large kitchen match with his thumbnail, and inhaled. He was one of the biggest men Ingram had ever seen, and he seemed to radiate an almost tangible aura of violence. Not evil, particularly—just violence. He had, in fact, an almost likable face, rugged and not unpleasantly ugly, spattered with the brown freckles and peeling sunburn of the heliophobe, and stamped with the casual recklessness of the utterly self-confident. His pale red hair was largely gone on top, showing a freckled expanse of scalp, though he was obviously not much over thirty. He wore nothing except unlaced shoes and a pair of khaki trousers hacked off at the knees.

The other man had rolled off the bunk and was standing near the foot of it with his back against the wall of boxes. He appeared to be in his early forties, and had a slender Latin face and grave brown eyes. He had shoved the Colt .45 automatic into the waistband of his trousers as if he were only a spectator. It was the big one who completely dominated the scene.

Rae Osborne looked around. "Where is the other man?"

"What other man?"

"Patrick Ives."

"Never heard of him," the big man said. He grinned at the Latin. "Carlos, you got the passenger list?"

"He was on here," Rae Osborne snapped. "Why lie about it? The dinghy was picked up, with his clothes and watch—"

"Oh, you mean Hollister."

"His name wasn't Hollister."

He gestured impatiently. "So who cares what his name was? He's dead. That's why we need Herman."

Ingram was thinking he'd been betrayed by his own narrow professional outlook as much as anything. Nobody had made an effort to get her off, hence there was nobody aboard. This possibility hadn't even occurred to him. He looked at the boxes, aware that at least they knew now why the *Dragoon* had been stolen. He should have guessed it before. "Where were you bound?" he asked. "Cuba?"

The big man shook his head. "Central America."

"You'd never make it, even if you got her off."

"We'll make it, don't worry."

"What does he mean?" Rae Osborne broke in. "And what's in all those boxes?"

"Guns," Ingram said.

"Knock it off," the big man ordered. "We can't stand here all day flapping our gums. We've got that plane to take care of. Take a squint, Carlos, and see where it is now."

The Latin turned and looked out one of the small portholes. "The same. About a mile."

"Facing this way?"

"More or less."

"All right, here's the shedule, as the Limeys say—"

"Listen," Ingram interrupted. "Whatever your name is—"

The big man laughed. "Did we forget to introduce ourselves? Wait'll the yacht club hears about that. I'm Al Morrison. And this is Carlos Ruiz."

"All right," Ingram said, "just what do you think you're going to do?"

Morrison shook his head. "That's exactly what I'm trying to tell you, if you'd shut up and listen. You're going up on top, you and the cupcake. That pilot'll be able to see you, but he couldn't hear you if you yelled your lungs out. You look everything over, give it the old expert routine, and then you come back down and get on the horn and tell the pilot to go home. You've decided you can get her loose from the mud, and you're going to stay aboard and sail her back to Key West."

"And then what?" Ingram asked.

"As soon as he gets out of sight, we go to work. You've just been elected vice president in charge of transportation."

He couldn't mean it, Ingram thought. He couldn't be that crazy. "Look, Morrison—use your head, will you? Running guns is one thing—"

Morrison cut him off. "Save it. I need legal advice, I'll send for a lawyer."

"We can't call the plane with this phone. They use different frequencies."

"Snow me not, Herman. I may not know my foot from a bale of hay about boats, but I do know something about radios and planes. Most of these crates in the Islands carry the intership frequencies. Carlos, you hold 'em till I get set."

"Okay," Ruiz said. He removed the automatic from the waistband of his khakis. Morrison went by them and disappeared into the passageway going forward. Even in the sloppy, unlaced shoes, he moved as though he were on pads.

"How about it, Ruiz?" Ingram demanded. "You want to spend the rest of your life in prison for a few lousy guns?"

Ruiz shrugged. "No spik Inglish."

Morrison called out forward. Ruiz motioned with the automatic. They went up the companion ladder and stood in the cockpit in brilliant sunlight. Ruiz was covering them from the ladder, his head still below the cockpit coaming. The forward hatch, just beyond the foremast, was slightly open, and he could see the muzzle of the BAR watching them like an unwinking eye. Smart, he thought. If they'd stayed below, Avery might conceivably have suspected something, but now it would appear from the plane they'd found nothing in the cabin and had returned to the deck to complete the inspection before calling.

"Stay over to the right," Morrison ordered. "Don't get behind those masts. Try to jump over the side, and I'll cut Dreamboat off at the knees."

"Well," Rae Osborne demanded, "does he think we're going to stand still for this?"

"He seems to," Ingram said.

"Aren't you going to do anything at all?"

He turned and looked at her. "Can you suggest something?"

Morrison called orders. They walked up the starboard side. He looked out at the plane, lying placidly on the ater a mile away like a child's toy on a mirror. It could ust as well be in another universe. They crossed to the ort side abaft the foremast and stared down in the water. What happened to Hollister?" he asked.

"He drowned," Morrison replied from the hatch.

"How?"

"Trying to swim back to the boat."

From the dinghy, he thought. "What was he doing? nd where did it happen?"

"Right here. We ran aground during the night, and the ext morning Hollister said we'd have to unload the guns » get her off. He took the skiff and went over to that ttle island to see if it was dry enough to stack 'em on. n the way back the motor quit on him. The tide was unning pretty fast, and he started to drift away. He took ff his clothes and jumped in and tried to kick it along ith his feet. He kept losing ground, though, and finally ft it and started to swim. He didn't make it."

"What day was this?"

"Sunday, I think. What difference does it make? Now ɔ back and start the engine."

They went aft. Ingram stepped down into the cockpit. he engine controls were beside the helmsman's station. e switched on the ignition, set the choke, and pressed the arter switch. On the third attempt, the engine fired ith a puff of exhaust smoke under the stern and settled ɔwn to a steady rumble that could easily be heard by very aboard the plane. Morrison might be crazy, but he asn't missing a bet.

"Turn it off. Go back down."

They went down the ladder. Ruiz backed up to the for-ard end of the cabin. Morrison emerged from the pas-geway between the two staterooms with the BAR slung . his arm. He nodded toward the radiotelephone. "Get ı the blower. Tell him just what I said."

Ingram shook his head. "No."

"Don't try to play tough, Herman. It could get real airy."

"You won't shoot."

"No. But I'll break Dreamboat's arm. We don't need r."

55

Silence fell, and tightened its grip on the scene. Ingram stared from one to the other. "I don't think you would."

Morrison regarded him with bitter humor. "That'd be kind of a tough one to second-guess, wouldn't it, Herman? This far from a doctor?"

He held it for another second. Once that plane was gone, it wouldn't be back. Morrison jerked his head at Rae Osborne. "Come here, baby."

Ruiz spoke then, in Spanish. "This I don't like, Alberto."

"Shut your mouth, you fool," Morrison snapped, also in perfect colloquial Spanish. "He may understand."

The suddenness of it caught Ingram by surprise. He fought to keep his face expressionless, hoping he'd recovered in time.

"He doesn't understand," Ruiz said. "And this thing is very bad."

He would break the arm, Morrison replied. Likewise the other arm. And he would commit other acts, which he detailed at some length. Spanish is a language of great beauty, but it also has potentialities for brutal and graphic obscenity probably surpassing even the Anglo-Saxon. Faint revulsion showed in Ruiz' eyes. Ingram believed he was being given an examination in the language, and managed to keep his face blank. He hoped Mrs. Osborne didn't speak it, or if she did, that she had learned it in school.

"See," Ruiz said. "It is as I have said. He does not understand. Must we do this?"

"We have no choice," Morrison snapped. "Would you like to go back?"

"It is unfortunate." Ruiz spread his hands. "Well, if we must—"

"What are you jabbering about?" Ingram demanded.

"Which one to break first, Herman," Morrison replied in English. "It's not a very pretty sound when it goes, but maybe she'll yell loud enough to cover it. Let's get on with it, Dreamboat." He stepped across, caught her wrist and began to bring it up behind her back.

"All right," Ingram said bleakly. "I'll call him."

56

Morrison smiled, and let go the wrist. "Now you're with . Just pick up the mike."

He lifted the handset from its cradle on the front of the strument. This actuated the switch starting the trans- itter; the converter whirred. Morrison had already set e band switch to 2638 Kc. He pressed the button. "This the *Dragoon,* calling McAllister plane." He didn't now the plane's call letters. *"Dragoon* to Avery, come , please."

There was a moment's tense silence. Then Avery's ice boomed in the loudspeaker. "Avery back to Captain gram. How does it look on there? Everything all right? ver."

Morrison nodded. Ingram spoke into the handset. Everything seems to be in good shape. I think we'll be le to kedge her off. We've decided to stay aboard and e if we can get her back to Key West. Over."

"You mean both of you?"

"Yes. Over."

Avery's voice came in. "I see. Well, if you run into any ouble and want us to come back or send a boat, call us rough the Miami Marine Operator. Can you get her ith your set?"

"Yes. We've got that channel."

"Good. Any sign of what happened to the thieves?"

Morrison shook his head, and made a rowing motion ith his left arm. Ingram looked bitterly around the bin. "No. Apparently they just abandoned her."

"Right. Well, if that's all, I'll take off. Good luck to u."

"Thanks. This is the *Dragoon,* off and clear."

He replaced the handset; the sound of the converter opped. What now? Apparently Avery had accepted Mrs. sborne's sudden change of mind without question. here'd been no mention of the money she still owed cAllister for the charter, but they would merely take it r granted she intended to pay as soon as they reached ey West. It could be as long as a week before anybody en began to wonder about it.

"What are you going to do with us? he asked.

"Nothing," Morrison replied. "You'll get your boat back when we're through with it."

"And when will that be?"

"As soon as we deliver the cargo."

"This is kidnap. You can get life for it. I don't think you're that dumb—"

"Shut up," Morrison ordered. "Go on top. I want you up there when he takes off."

They went up the ladder and stood on the after deck beside the cockpit with just the muzzle of the gun showing in the hatch behind them. "Don't look around this way," Morrison warned. They stared out at the plane. One of the propellers turned, shattering the sunlight, and then the cough and roar of the engine came to them across the mile of water. The other engine caught. The plane began to taxi toward the south. Ruiz is afraid of it, he thought. But that was no help; Morrison was in command, and he was the dangerous one. Well, he still had one small edge; they didn't know he spoke Spanish.

The plane had stopped now; it swung about, facing north. The engines roared and it began to gather speed. It went past them over a mile to the westward, lifted from the water, and began to dwindle away in the void. He felt sick. Morrison came up the ladder behind them, followed by Ruiz.

Morrison sat down on the corner of the deckhouse with the BAR across his legs, and said, "All right, let's get this scow off the mud. What do we do first?"

"Jettison those guns," Ingram said coldly.

"Come again with the jettison?"

"Throw 'em over the side."

"Don't bug me, Herman. The guns go on that island—"

Ruiz broke in suddenly, in Spanish. "Look! The plane returns."

Ingram caught himself, but too late. He'd already turned to look. He saw Morrison's jocose grin, and was filled with a dark and futile rage. That swept the series he'd been made a fool of by all three of them—Hollister, Morrison, and now Ruiz.

But it hadn't been a deliberate trick; the plane was turning and coming back. "Hit the dirt!" Morrison barked

58

He grabbed the gun and ducked down the hatch after Ruiz. Ingram watched it silently. Maybe Avery did suspect something. But it was turning again now, in a steep bank only a few hundred feet above the water some miles to the north of them. It was as though Avery was trying to see something below him. At that moment the radio blared in the cabin. Morrison spoke from the hatchway. "Get on the horn. He's calling you."

He ran down the ladder. Morrison had already started the transmitter. He passed over the handset and stood to one side, holding the gun. "Careful what you say, and watch me."

He pressed the transmit button. "This is the *Dragoon* back. What is it? Over."

Avery's voice filled the cabin. "There's something in the water down here. Hold it a minute. I'm coming over again."

They waited in tense, hot silence unbroken except for the scratching of static in the loudspeaker. Rae Osborne watched from the hatchway. Then Avery's voice came on again. "It's a body, all right. Probably one of your thieves. Seems to be naked except for a pair of shorts. If you bring the raft, I can land and get him aboard."

He glanced at Morrison. "Tell him you'll pick him up," the latter ordered, "and take him into Key West."

He repeated this.

"Very well," Avery agreed. "Might save a bit of international red tape, at that. I make the position about three miles north-northeast of you. If you get here while the water's still flat, you won't have any trouble finding him. There are some birds sitting on him."

He saw Mrs. Osborne shudder at the image. Morrison gave a curt gesture that said: *Get rid of him.* He signed off, and replaced the handset. When they went on deck again, the plane was fading away in the northeast.

Morrison perched on the corner of the deckhouse once more. "Now, how many of those guns do we have to unload?"

Rae Osborne stared at him. "But what about the man?"

Morrison shrugged. "So what about him?"

"Aren't we going to do anything at all?"

59

"Like giving him artificial respiration, maybe? He's only been dead for three days."

She took a step toward him, the green eyes blazing. "I've got to see him."

"A waterlogged stiff? Honey, you need help."

"Listen," Ingram said, "it won't take more than thirty minutes to row out there and see if she can identify him. She may know who Hollister was."

Morrison shook his head. "Fall back, Herman. I couldn't care less who Hollister was, and we've got more to do than stooge around the ocean looking for him."

"I'm going out there," Rae Osborne said. She started past him toward the raft, and violence erupted in the sunlit morning like the release of coiled steel springs.

Morrison caught the front of her pullover, yanked her toward him, and slapped her back-handed across the face. She gasped and tried to hit him. Ingram lunged at him just as he drew back his arm and shoved, sending her sprawling along the deck. Ruiz' arm flashed down swinging the slablike automatic. Pain exploded inside his head and he fell forward against Morrison, who stood up, pushed him off with the BAR, and chopped a short and brutal right to the side of his jaw. His knees buckled and he fell beside Mrs. Osborne. When he tried to get up, the deck tilted and spun, and there was no strength in his arms. He dropped back. Blood trickled down across his forehead and fell to the deck in little spatting droplets just under his eyes.

"Don't ever try that again, Herman," Morrison said. "You're a big boy, but we're in the business."

6

In a moment he was able to sit up, wincing with the pain in his head. Rae Osborne had pushed to a sitting position with her feet on the cockpit cushions. She had an inflamed red spot on the side of her face, and there were tears of frustration and rage in her eyes. "You're not much help," she said.

He mopped at the blood on his face with a handkerchief, but succeeded only in smearing it. He threw the handkerchief overboard. A vagrant breath of air riffled the water astern and a gull wheeled and cried out above them in the brassy sunlight. This was about as helpless as you could get, he thought; he'd lasted less than three seconds.

Morrison spoke to Ruiz. "As soon as the Champ's able to row that raft, we get started. Go down and begin taking the lashings off those cases."

Ruiz went down the ladder. "How much will we have to unload?" Morrison asked.

Ingram stared coldly. "How would I know?"

"You're the expert."

"I don't even know what you've got aboard. Or where the tide was when you piled up here."

"I don't know about the tide, but I can tell you what's aboard. Six hundred rifles, thirty machine guns, fifty BAR's, a half dozen mortars——"

"I don't need an inventory. I mean tonnage. Have you got any idea what it weighs?"

Morrison thought for a moment. "The ammo'd be the heaviest. We've got over a hundred thousand rounds of thirty-caliber stuff in those two staterooms. I'd guess it all at six to eight tons."

Ingram made a rough calculation based on a water-line

61

length of fifty-five feet and a beam amidships of sixteen. Call it thirty-five cubic feet displacement per inch of draft at normal water line. Each ton would put her down nearly another full inch. No wonder she'd looked low in the water.

"You've got her overloaded at least six inches. If you'd hit any weather she could have foundered or broken her back."

"Never mind that jazz. How much do we take off."

"Probably all of it. How long have you been on here?"

"Since Saturday night."

"And this is Wednesday. She's never moved at all?"

"No," Morrison said.

"Has the tide ever come any higher than it is now?"

"How would I know?" Morrison asked. "You think we got anything to measure it with?"

"Use your head. Has the deck ever been any nearer level than it is right now?"

"No. This is about it."

"Then congratulations. Apparently you plowed on here at full speed on the highest tide of the month."

"So what do we do, sit here and cry? Let's get going."

"If you were bound for the Caribbean, why were you on a northerly heading when you hit?"

Morrison gestured impatiently. "We were trying to turn to get out of here. It was night, like I said, and we couldn't see anything. And all of a sudden we heard something that sounded like a beach."

"You turned the wrong way. But I don't get what you were doing in here over the Bank in the first place. You should have been at least ten miles to the westward."

"I wouldn't know about that. I'm no navigator. It looks like we could have used one. I tried to get Hollister to proposition you—"

"Wait a minute. You mean you know me?"

"Sure. I thought I recognized you when you came aboard, and when the pilot called you Ingram I had you made."

"Where did you see me before?"

"In the lobby of the Eden Roc when you went to see Hollister the first time."

Rae Osborne broke in. "Why did this man Hollister want somebody else to inspect the *Dragoon* instead of going himself?"

Morrison shrugged. "He said the watchman might remember him. He was an old boy friend of the owner, and he'd been aboard before."

She said nothing, and turned to stare out across the water to the northward. Well, at least her question was answered, Ingram thought. "Whose idea was it, stealing the boat?" he asked.

"Hollister's. Or whatever you said his name was."

"Patrick Ives," she said.

"Anyway, he was supposed to furnish the transportation and the know-how to get us down there. Said he'd been around boats a lot, and used to be a navigator in the Eighth Air Force during the war. From the looks of it, he wasn't so hot. We could have used you."

"You did," Ingram said. "That's why I'm here. Where did you get the guns?"

"We stole 'em."

"All right, I'll make you a proposition," Ingram said. "I think I can get this schooner afloat when those guns are off. So we throw them over the side and take the schooner back to Key West. They're contraband. Nobody can claim them legally, so there'll be no charge against you except for stealing the boat. I think Mrs. Osborne'll agree not to press that, if she gets the boat back undamaged, so probably the worst you'd get would be a suspended sentence."

"Nothing doing. We're going to deliver the guns."

The throbbing in his head was agony, and he had to close his eyes against the glare of the sun. What was the matter with the stupid muscle-head; wasn't there any way you could make him understand? He fought down an impulse to shout. "Listen, Morrison," he said wearily, "try to use your head, will you? You're not in a serious jam yet, but if you go through with this you haven't got a chance. You'll be facing a federal charge of kidnaping. They'll run you down and put you away for life."

"Not me. I'll be long gone."

"You think you're going to hide out in Latin America? Did you ever take a look at yourself?"

"It's easy when you speak the language and you've got money and connections."

"Not when they want you for something big back here. The U.S. State Department's got connections too."

Morrison's eyes began to grow ugly. "I'm not asking you about this, pal. I'm telling you. We're going to put those guns on that island. When we get the boat loose, we bring 'em back."

Ingram looked out toward the narrow strip of sand. "The raft won't carry over a couple of hundred pounds at a time. It'll take the rest of the week."

"No, I've already got it figured out. We won't have to ferry 'em all the way. The water looks shallow over there. You haul 'em to where I can wade out and meet you, and I take 'em from there while you come back for another load. Like a bucket brigade. Now let's get going." He stood up and called down the hatchway. "You all set, Carlos?"

"The ropes are off the left side," Ruiz replied from below. "I'm starting on the right."

Ingram looked out at the surface of the water and could see the faint beginnings of movement. The tide had passed high slack and was starting to ebb slowly past the imprisoned hull. Well, let him go ahead and kill himself, he thought; it'd be one less to contend with. Then he shrugged uncomfortably, and knew he couldn't do it; it wasn't Ruiz' fault.

"You'd better tell your boy not to take the lashings off the starboard side," he said to Morrison. "Not till he's got room to unpile those cases."

"Why?" Morrison asked.

"The tide's started to drop. About two more degrees of port list and you'll have to bring him out of there in a basket."

"Yeah, I guess you're right at that. Youse is a good boy, Herman. Maybe we'll put you on permanent."

"Go to hell," he said. "If it'd been you, I wouldn't have said anything."

He walked aft to the helmsman's station while Morrison was talking to Ruiz. Something still didn't quite ring true; they shouldn't have been in here over the Bank. He stood frowning at the binnacle. He stepped down into the cockpit, removed the hood, and checked the heading on the compass. The lubber line lay at 008 degrees. There was no compass-deviation card posted anywhere that he could see.

Rae Osborne came aft and stood beside him. "What are we going to do?"

"Just what he says, from the looks of it."

"Maybe there'll be a search for us."

Probably not until it was too late to do any good, Ingram thought, but he said nothing. There was no point in scaring her. She probably didn't realize how sad this situation was, anyway. Even if they managed to refloat the schooner, their troubles were only beginning. The *Dragoon* was dangerously overloaded, her trim and buoyancy destroyed; in anything except perfect weather, she could founder and go down like a dropped brick. And as for landing a cargo of guns on a hostile coast— His thoughts broke off. She was staring out at the empty horizon to the northward. Well, the chances were a million to one nobody would ever see Ives again, now that the tide had turned and the body was floating seaward.

"All right, Herman, let's go," Morrison called out. They went forward to the break of the deckhouse. Ruiz was pushing one of the wooden crates up the companion ladder into the cockpit. Morrison had put on a shirt and a soft straw hat and carried a gallon jug of water in his other hand. "You take me across first," he said, "and then start bringing the rifles. They're packed ten to a crate, so each crate'll go a little over a hundred pounds. The raft ought to carry two at a trip. Dreamboat, you stay here in the cockpit and guide 'em up the ladder for Ruiz. And don't bother trying to get to that radio when he's not looking. We took some of the tubes out of it."

He gestured with the gun. Any further argument was useless. Ingram stepped down into the raft and passed up his suitcase and Rae Osborne's purse. Morrison got in and seated himself aft with the BAR across his legs while Ingram cast off the painter. They rowed up the side of the schooner and around the bow. The narrow sand spit ran north and south, its nearest point some three hundred yards off the starboard bow. The channel of slightly deeper water which ran astern of the schooner and westward toward the edge of the Bank continued on around and up the starboard side approximately a hundred yards away, passing between the schooner and the western edge of the spit. Beyond the channel the water appeared to shoal abruptly, judging from its color, extending in a wide and barely submerged flat on all sides of the dry ridge.

There was still no wind. The water lay flat as oil, reflecting the metallic glare of the sun. The day was going to be like the inside of a furnace, Ingram thought; and in a little over an hour the tide would be running out across here at two or three knots. He wondered if Morrison had even thought of that. Probably not; he seemed to be in the grip of obsession and incapable of seeing obstacles at all. They crossed the channel, and the sandy bottom began to come up toward them. Morrison was peering down into the water. "Hold it," he ordered. He slid his legs over and stood up; the water was only waist deep. They were still a little over a hundred yards from dry ground, and it was approximately twice that far back to the schooner.

"All right," he said. "Start bringing 'em over."

Ingram turned and rowed back toward the *Dragoon*. The big man waded on ashore through progressively shallower water, put the BAR and his bottle of water on the sand, and stood watching. The pain in Ingram's head had subsided to a dull throbbing, but the dried blood made his face feel stiff and caked. He dipped up water and washed it while he coldly sized up their chances of escape. You couldn't give them much. How about trying for it in the raft? The BAR was a short-range weapon and not very accurate at this distance, so if they could give Ruiz the slip— No. The nearest land was the west coast of Andros, seventy-five miles away, and even if they made it before they choked to death on their tongues, they were still nowhere. There were no settlements on that side, nothing but swamp and mosquitoes and a maze of stagnant and forbidding waterways; they'd never get across the island. Forget the raft. They had to take the schooner. Play for

Ruiz, he thought; they'd be working together loading the crates onto the raft. Watch for a chance to yank him overboard and make him lose the gun.

He came alongside. Ruiz had four cases out of the cabin now, stacked on deck beside the forward end of the cockpit with their ends projecting outward. The Latin himself was standing in the cockpit behind them with the .45 stuck in his trousers.

Ingram caught one of the lifeline stanchions. "Give me a hand."

Ruiz shook his head. "You don't need any help."

"So. A general."

"Go ahead. Slide them down."

"*El Libertador* himself. It's too bad we haven't got a horse so you could pose for an equestrian statue."

Ruiz looked bored. "Put away the needle, Ingram. You're wasting your time."

Apparently he'd guarded prisoners before. It didn't look very promising.

"*Cómo está la cabeza?*" Ruiz asked.

So he couldn't resist the temptation to do a little needling of his own, Ingram thought. "The head is nothing, my General," he replied in Spanish. "In the great cause of freedom, I spit on all discomfort. But let us consider the General's neck. How does it stretch?"

"Shut up and start moving those crates," Ruiz said in English, "before you get another lump on your head."

Ingram shrugged, and began easing one of the boxes down into the raft. It was an awkward maneuver, but he managed it without capsizing. He slid another down beside it. They lay between his outstretched feet and projected out over the stern.

"Will it carry another?" Ruiz asked.

"See for yourself, *cabrón*." The raft was down by the stern, and cranky. One more would make it unmanageable or capsize it.

"Okay. Get going."

He rowed up around the bow of the schooner and across the channel. Morrison had waded out again, without the gun, and was standing in waist-deep water waiting for him. The shirt stretched across his massive chest and shoulders was wet with sweat. "Shake it up, Herman. You're taking too long."

"This is not my idea," Ingram replied coldly.

"Never mind your idea. Try dragging your feet, and you'll get worked over with a gun barrel." He heaved one of the crates over his left shoulder, took the other under his arm, and went plowing across the flat toward dry ground. As if they were empty, Ingram thought. He looked at his watch; it was seven minutes past eight. At the end of the next round trip he checked the time again and saw it had taken eleven minutes. Call it five trips an hour. Two hundred pounds each time—that would mean at least fourteen hours to move seven tons. And just one way. They'd still have to wait for the next tide, try to get her off, and bring it all back. And he was clocking it at slack water; wait'll that tide started to run.

On the next trip, while Morrison was picking up the crates, he said, "This'll take three days, at the minimum."

The big man scarcely paused. "So?"

"She'll never make it across the Caribbean, anyway. She's overloaded."

"This is June; she'll make it. Hollister said so."

"Sure. He said he could navigate, too. And look where you are."

"Shut up and get going."

An hour went by. The current was picking up now as the tide ebbed westward off the bank; with each trip it became worse. By ten o'clock perspiration was running from his body and his arms ached from the battle with the oars. It was the loaded trip that was the killer; he was quartering across the current with the raft low in the water, and he had to point farther and farther upstream in order to make it before he was swept away to the west of the sand spit. In another half hour he had to row straight upstream from the schooner until he was above Morrison, and then turn across. It took fifteen minutes of furiously paced rowing, during which a slow or missed beat meant losing ground already gained. When Morrison caught hold of the raft, water was running past his legs.

Ingram looked at him through the blur of sweat in his

eyes. "That's it until the tide slacks. Unless you want to do it."

Morrison nodded. "I see what you mean. We'll knock off and have a sandwich. Hold it here till I get back."

Ingram stepped out and held the raft while the big man carried the two crates ashore; it was easier than doing it with the oars, and he couldn't get any wetter than he was already. Morrison came back carrying the BAR, and got in. "That makes twenty-four," he said.

A little over a ton, Ingram thought; they'd barely started. He rowed back to the *Dragoon*. When he stepped aboard, the cramped leg gave way under him, and he had to grab a lifeline to keep from falling. A light breeze had come up at mid-morning, but it had died away again, and the deck was blistering under the brutal weight of the sun. Rae Osborne's face was flushed, and tendrils of hair were plastered to her forehead as she collapsed on the cushions in the cockpit. Not far from a case of heat prostration or sunstroke, he thought. And there was no escape from the sun; below decks would be unbearable.

"There's an awning down in the sail locker," he told Morrison. "If you thought you could take that gun out of my back for five minutes, I'd bring it up and rig it."

"Go ahead," Morrison said.

He went down the forward hatch with Ruiz watching him from above. There were three bunks in the narrow cabin just forward of the galley, with suitcases and scattered articles of clothing on two of them. He opened the small access door to the locker in the eyes of the ship and looked around in stifling semi-darkness among coils of line and bags of spare sails until he found the awning. He boosted it up the hatch to Ruiz, then carried it aft and rigged it above the cockpit. The air was still far from cool beneath it, but it did offer shelter from the pitiless glare of the sun. They sat down, with Morrison perched on the corner of the deckhouse holding the BAR. It's an extension of his personality, Ingram thought; he probably never feels comfortable without it.

"Who wants a sandwich?" Morrison asked.

Ingram shook his head; it was too hot to eat anything. "Makes me sick at my stomach to think about it," Rae

Osborne said. She sat up and dug listlessly in her purse for a cigarette.

Ruiz went below and returned a few minutes later with two sandwiches. He and Morrison ate in silence. Morrison threw the remainder of his overboard, watched it float away on the tide, and set the gun behind him on the deckhouse. "Mind the store," he said to Ruiz, and went below. Ingram looked at the gun. Ruiz intercepted the glance, and shook his head, the slim Latin face devoid of any expression whatever. It was useless, Ingram knew. They were a team, and a good one, in the skilled profession of violence—whatever their particular branch of it was.

When Morrison returned he was carrying a tall glass containing some colorless fluid and three ice cubes. Rae Osborne looked at it with interest. "What's that?"

"Rum," he said.

"Is there any more?"

"Whole case of it, Toots. You'll have to use water, though. We're out of Cokes."

She brightened visibly. "You've convinced me. Which way's the bar?"

"Straight ahead till you come to a room full of dirty dishes. Bottle's on the sink, reefers under it. Bring Herman one while you're at it."

"I don't want any," Ingram said.

She disappeared below. Well, maybe that was the practical attitude; if you couldn't whip 'em, join 'em, especially if they had anything to drink. He removed the soggy leather case from his shirt, found a cigar that might be dry enough to burn, and lighted it. He stepped back to the binnacle, removed the hood, and looked at the compass again. The heading had changed to 012. He nodded thoughtfully. Rae Osborne came up the ladder, carrying her drink, and sat down with her feet stretched out across the cockpit.

"This is more like it," she said to Morrison. "What about these guns? Where are you going with them?"

"A place called Bahía San Felipe, just north of the Canal."

"You going to start a revolution, or what?"

70

Morrison shook his head. "We're just supplying the uff this time."

"How did Patrick Ives get mixed up in it? It's a little ut of his line."

Morrison chuckled. "Money. That's in his line, isn't it?"

"Yes. I think you could say that. And then say it again. ut just how did you meet?"

"I ran into him in a bar in Miami two or three weeks go. We got to talking about gun-running, among other ings. It was a big business around there for a while dur- g the Cuban fracas, you remember, and the Feds were ill uncovering a batch now and then. Anyway, I hap- ned to mention I knew where there was a whole ship- ent hid out in an old house down near Homestead——"

"How did you know about it?" Rae Osborne asked.

"From one of the boys that'd been flying it in for this articular outfit. I was in the racket myself, and knew ite a few of 'em. Anyway, this Hollister—or Ives as you ll him—got interested in it and wanted to know what I ought the shipment was worth. I told him probably a ndred grand—that is, delivered to somebody that eded it bad enough. So he wanted to know if it would possible to lift the stuff and maybe peddle it some- here. I told him getting away with it would be a cinch, t that there wasn't much market for it at present. Then remembered Carlos. We'd been in a couple of Central merican revolutions together, besides the Cuban one, d he knew most of the politicos-in-exile that Miami's ways full of, and could probably come up with a cus- mer if we could figure out a way to deliver. That's when es got the idea of liberating the *Dragoon*. He said he uld sail it, and knew how to navigate. The only trouble as, it'd been some time since he'd been aboard the boat, d he didn't know what kind of condition it was in— turally, we couldn't steal it and then go in a shipyard mewhere—so we'd have to look it over first. He couldn't himself because the watchman might recognize him and ow the whistle on him afterward, and Carlos and I dn't know anything about boats, so we had to send some- dy else."

Rae Osborne took another sip of her drink. "Do the

people who owned the guns know who got away with them?"

Morrison shook his head. "Not a chance. We took 'em out of the house at night with a truck we rented under a phony name."

"How did you get them aboard the *Dragoon?*"

"We brought her into a place down in the Keys after dark and put 'em aboard with a couple of skiffs, along with the supplies and gasoline we'd picked up at different places. We spent the rest of the night slapping a coat of paint on her, and got out just before daylight. That was still before anybody even realized she was stolen."

"And you're still determined to deliver the guns?"

"Of course."

"How long do you think it'll take?"

"Less than two weeks. After we get loose here, I mean. What do you think, Herman?"

"It would depend on the weather," Ingram said. "And to a great extent on whether you ever got there at all."

"You've got a negative attitude, pal. Learn to look on the bright side."

Rae Osborne shrugged, and drained her glass. "Well, I'd have given odds I'd never be in the gun-running business, but I guess you never know. I think we ought to have another one."

"Sure." Morrison grinned. "I'll go with you. I could use one too."

They went down the ladder. In a moment the sound of laughter issued from below. Ingram puffed his cigar and tried to read Ruiz' expression, but it was inscrutable. He knows it, though, he thought; we're headed for more trouble, if we didn't have enough already. The two of them came back shortly with fresh drinks.

"You're sure I get the *Dragoon* back?" she asked.

"Natch. What do I want with it? As soon as the guns are off and we get paid, Carlos and I take it on the Arthur Duffy, and you and Herman can sail it back to Key West. We'll see you get enough supplies and fresh water for the trip. What's to complain about—a Caribbean cruise, with me along as social director? Hell, if we'd advertised, we'd have had to fight the girls off with clubs."

72

She laughed. "You know what I like about you? It's your modesty."

Ingram looked at her with disgust, thinking that boredom must be a terrible thing. She was already telling people about it at cocktail parties. *All the way across the Caribbean, darling, with this whole load of guns and bullets and stuff that might blow up any minute or something, and this absolute brute of a man that looked like Genghis Khan except he was kind of cute in a hairy sort of way if you know what I mean, and always carrying this awful machine gun in his arm . . .* It was just a lark, like trying to get an extra carton of cigarettes past the Customs inspector.

He wondered if it would do any good to tell her the chances were excellent she'd never even get across the Caribbean in a boat loaded as the *Dragoon* was, and that if she did and was lucky enough not to be killed outright by the Guarda Costas she'd probably have her boat confiscated and spend several years in a verminous prison where the United States State Department couldn't do anything for her at all. Then he shrugged. It didn't seem worth the effort.

7

By 12:30 p.m. the outgoing tide had slowed enough to permit resumption of the unloading operation. The work went on through the blistering heat of afternoon. The tide was at slack low shortly after two, with the *Dragoon's* list at its most pronounced. Ingram's shoulders ached, and he lost count of the number of trips he had made. On the sand spit, the pile of boxes grew larger hour by hour. The tide began to flood. By five p.m. the current was again becoming a problem, and at a little before six Morrison called a halt and rode the raft back to the *Dragoon*.

"That's all the rifles," he said, as they sat in the cockpit in their dripping clothes. "Let's see—sixty times a hundred . . ."

Three tons off, Ingram thought. The schooner's list was decreasing now by slow degrees as the tide rose, and it should be about two hours more until slack high. It would be interesting to see how far she might be from floating then, but he was almost too tired to care. Ruiz brought up a plate of sandwiches and they ate on deck while sunset died beyond the Santaren Channel in a thundering orchestration of color. Ingram watched it, remembering other tropical sunsets down the long roll of the years and wondering how many were left now in his own personal account. Probably not many, from the looks of things at the moment. He couldn't see any way out, and all he could do was go on waiting for something to break.

But what? he wondered. Even if Morrison took off that prosthetic BAR when he went to sleep, which appeared unlikely, he was still no match for the man in a fight. Not now, at forty-three—and the chances were he never had been. And there was always Ruiz and his Colt. There was something a little mad, he thought, in this harping on those two guns when the *Dragoon*'s whole cargo consisted of a hundred-thousand-dollar assortment of deadly weapons, but they were all crated and out of reach, and the ammunition for them was crated separately.

He was roused from the quiet futility of his thoughts by a shrill laugh from Rae Osborne. She and Morrison were dipping into the rum again, and apparently Morrison had just said something very funny. He let his gaze slide past their oasis of alcoholic gaiety to where Ruiz sat cross-legged atop the deckhouse, and this time the grave imperturbability of the mask had slipped a little and he could see, in addition to the Spanish contempt for drunkenness, the growing shadow of concern. Ruiz knew him, so that probably meant he was inclined to get pretty goaty and unbuttoned among the grapes. You had to admit they had all the ingredients for a memorable cruise—a boisterous giant, an arsenal of weapons, plenty of rum, and a bored and stupid woman apparently bent on agitating the mixture to see what would happen.

"Maybe Herman'd like a drink," Morrison said.

Rae Osborne shrugged. "Herman's not stapled to the deck. Let him go get one."

Morrison lighted a cigarette and spoke to Ruiz. "We better figure out what we're going to do with 'em tonight, unless we want to take turns standing watch. Tie 'em up, or lock 'em in one of those staterooms?"

"It's pretty stuffy down there till after midnight," Ruiz said. "Why not put them on the island? They can't get off as long as we've got the raft."

"Sure, that'd do it. Leftenant, you're now a captain."

Rae Osborne rattled the ice in her glass and said sulkily, "You mean I've got to go over on that crummy sand bar and sleep on the ground like Daniel Boone? I want another drink first."

"Sure, Baby Doll. Have all you want."

"Besides, what could I do to that hunk of brute force, anyway? You afraid I might overpower you, or something?"

Morrison grinned. "On second thought, maybe we'll reconsider the first thought. Our yacht is your yacht. Drink up."

"Open another bottle, Commodore, and alert the riot squad. Can you get any mambo music on that radio?"

Ruiz stood up and spoke to Ingram. "You ready to go?"

"Yes," Ingram said. He looked at Rae Osborne. "You're sure you want to stay?"

She considered this thoughtfully. "If I have your permission, Herman. Tell you what—you go check the action on that sand bar, and if it's real frantic, drop me a line."

Morrison spread his hands. "Looks like you lose, Herman."

"I guess so," Ingram said. "Anyway, it's one interpretation."

Rae Osborne smiled. "Don't mind Captain Ingram. He's full of deep remarks like that. He's a philosopher. With corners, that is."

Ingram nodded curtly to Ruiz. "Let's go."

He took the oars while Ruiz sat in the stern holding the Colt. It was dusk now, and the flow of the tide was decreasing as it approached high slack. The sand spit was a low, dark shadow marked by the pale gleam of the boxes where Morrison had stacked them near the southern end. Neither of them said anything until the raft grounded in the shallows beyond the channel. Ingram got out. Ruiz moved over and took the oars. *"Buenas noches."*

"Buenas noches," Ingram said. The raft moved away in the thickening twilight, and he waded ashore to stand for a moment beside the piled boxes, savoring the unbroken quiet and the clean salt smell of solitude and night. Then some faint remnant of deep-water surge flattened by miles of shoals and bars curled forward and died with a gentle slap against the sand, and somewhere beyond him in the darkness a cruising barracuda slashed at bait. Everybody, he supposed, had something he hated above all else to leave, and this was his: the tropic sea. In a dozen lifetimes he'd never have grown tired of it.

The bottle of water was near his feet. He picked it up, and judged it was still half full. He wondered how many cigars he had, wishing he'd thought to get more from his suitcase before leaving the schooner, but when he opened the case and probed with his fingers he discovered he had three. That was plenty. He lighted one and sat down on the sand with his back against the boxes.

Could he get aboard later on when they would be asleep? He could swim that far, but getting onto the schooner would be something else. They'd be too smart to leave the raft in the water so he could climb into it and reach the deck. How about the bobstay? He should be able to reach the lower end of that and work his way hand over hand up to the bowsprit. But the chances of doing it without waking either of them were admittedly dim; at any rate, he'd have to wait until after midnight.

A shriek of laughter reached his ears, and then the sound of music. They'd switched on the all-wave radio. He lay back on the sand and watched the slow wheel of the constellations while the sound of revelry came to him across the night. For a while he pictured the inevitable progress of the brawl, but gave it up with the accumulation of disgust and tried to shut it out. It was none of his business. His thoughts broke off then as he caught the

76

sound of oars. He heard the raft scrape on sand, and stood up. The slender figure would be Ruiz. It waded ashore in the starlit darkness and pulled the raft onto the beach. He appeared to be carrying something in his arm.

"Over here," Ingram said quietly.

"Don't try to get behind me, *amigo*."

"I'm not," Ingram replied. He flicked on the cigar lighter. "Party get a little rough for you?"

Ruiz came into the circle of light, the fatal olive face as expressionless as ever. "I brought you some bedding," he said, dropping a blanket and pillow on the sand. "Gets a little cool out here before morning."

"Thanks a lot," Ingram said. "Sit down and talk for a while. You smoke cigars?"

"I've got cigarettes, thanks." He took one out and lighted it, squatting on his heels just precisely out of reach with the eternal vigilance of the professional. A shellburst of maracas and Cuban drums came to them across the water. *"Están bailando,"* he said with faint reluctance, as though he felt he should say something of the party but wished to make it as little as possible. Well, if they were dancing, Ingram thought, the brawl must be still on a more or less vertical plane. He wondered what difference it made.

"What kind of guy is Morrison?" he asked.

"Rugged. And very smart."

"How long have you known him?"

"Off and on, since the war. We were in New Guinea together, and later sent in with a kind of shaggy and irregular outfit in the Philippines. On that guerrilla stuff, he could write the book."

"That where he learned Spanish?"

"Yes, but not during the war. He was born in the Philippines; his father was in the mining business. But he has the knack—some people have it, some don't. He also speaks Tagalog and German and a couple of very useless Central American Indian dialects. And Beatnik. Incidentally, where did you learn it?"

"Mexico, and Puerto Rico. But my accent's not as good as his."

"No," Ruiz said.

"Where are you from?"

"Here and there. I went to school in the States."

"U.S. citizen?"

"Yes. Since the war."

He fell silent. Ingram waited. He hadn't come out here merely to exchange biographical information. Maybe, with the Spaniard's innate dislike for drunkenness, he was just escaping from the party, but he could have something else on his mind.

"How far are we from the coast of Cuba?" Ruiz asked then.

"Hundred miles," Ingram said. "Maybe a little less. Why?"

"I just wondered. What would you say were the chances of making it in that raft?"

"How many people?"

"Call it one."

"Still very dim, even with one. It's too small."

"That's what I thought. But when we get started again, if we do, we pass pretty close, don't we?"

"That's right. The way into the Caribbean from here is through the Windward Passage between Cuba and Haiti. You'll be within sight of Cape Maysi."

"Maysi?"

"*Punta Maisí*. It's the eastern tip of Cuba."

"I get the picture."

He's going over the hill, Ingram thought. But why? They've got it all their way at the moment. Something nibbled at the edge of memory, and then was gone. "What's the trouble?" he asked. He wouldn't get the truth, but he might get one of the wrong answers he could eliminate.

"This is a sad operation," Ruiz said. "And getting sadder. We'll never make it."

"There is that chance. And a very good one. But then I wouldn't say that knife-and-run stuff in the Philippines was anything that'd make you popular with insurance companies."

"Maybe I was younger then. When you're nineteen, it's always somebody else that's going to get it."

78

What is it? Ingram thought. "You worried about the booze?"

"Sure. Aren't you?"

So that wasn't it.

"How about a deal?" Ingram asked.

"No deal." The voice was quiet, but there was finality in it.

"Stealing a boat's not such a terrible charge. Especially if the owner doesn't want to press it."

"No," Ruiz said. "I told you we'd been friends a long time."

"But you're looking for a way out."

"That's different. If you don't like the action, you can always walk out. You don't have to sell out."

"Okay, have it your way," Ingram said. He leaned back against the boxes. "This Ives—what kind of guy was he?"

"He wasn't a bad sort of Joe if you didn't believe too much of what he said. He talked a good game."

"So I gather," Ingram said.

There was a moment's silence, and then he asked, "By the way, where's the deviation card for the compass? Do you know?"

"The what?" Ruiz asked.

"It's a correction card you make out for compass error. You did make a new one, didn't you, when you swung ship?"

"Swung ship? What for? I think you've lost me, friend."

"To adjust compass," Ingram explained. "Look—you did swing it, didn't you?"

"Not that I know of."

"You mean you loaded three or four tons of steel down in that cabin and it didn't occur to you it might have some effect on the compass?"

"Oh, that. Sure, we knew about it. You wouldn't have to be a sailor. Any Boy Scout would know it. Anyway, Ives took care of it."

"How?" Ingram asked.

"He took a bearing on something ashore before we loaded the guns, and then another one afterward. What-

79

ever the difference was, he wrote it down somewhere. A
probably knows where it is."

"I see," Ingram said quietly. "Well, I'll ask him abou
it."

Ruiz slid the glowing end of his cigarette into the sanc
and stood up. "Guess I'll go back and see if I can ge
some sleep. I hope."

"Hasta mañana," Ingram said. He started to get up.

"No," Ruiz said in his cool, ironic voice. "Don't bothe:
following me to the door."

"Okay. About Ives—did he ever actually tell you tha
was his name?"

"No. I figured Hollister was phony, of course, but that':
the only way I knew him. That and Fred."

"What did Morrison call him?"

"Herman. What else?"

"Excuse a stupid question," Ingram said. "Thanks fo:
the bedding."

"De nada," Ruiz said. He melted into the darkness.

Ingram leaned back against the boxes and relighted hi:
cigar. Somebody was lying, that was for certain. But who'
The thing was so mixed up and the possibilities so endless
you couldn't put your finger on where it had to be. Why
did Ruiz want out? That stuff about being afraid of th
trip was almost certainly a smoke screen. That is, unles'
he knew of some other danger Ingram himself hadn'
learned of yet—something that made death or capture ar
absolute certainty instead of merely another chance yo
took. He was a professional soldier of fortune who'd livec
along the edge of violence since his teens; he didn't scar€
that easily, at nineteen or thirty-nine.

But there was another possibility. Could there be some
thing unnatural in the Morrison-Ruiz relationship, ir
which case it was Rae Osborne who'd thrown the dunga
rees in the chowder? No, he decided; that was ridiculous
Deviation wasn't necessarily accompanied by the limj
wrist and effeminate mannerisms, but you nearly alway
sensed it, and there was none of it here. He was glac
somehow; in spite of the circumstances, Ruiz was a mar
you could like. He'd been opposed to this thing from th€

beginning, and if he hadn't been overruled by Morrison—

ngram sat up abruptly. There it was.

Would you like to go back?

That was the thing he'd almost remembered a while

go. It was what Morrison had said in Spanish before they

ealized he understood the language, the thing that had

topped Ruiz' protests.

So they couldn't go back.

But why? Because of the charge of theft? It had to be

1ore than that. Were they afraid of the men from whom

hey'd stolen the guns? That might be it, of course, but he

ad a feeling it was still something more. Then it occurred

2 him that this didn't really answer the question, anyway.

Ruiz' problem wasn't simply that he couldn't go back; for

2me reason he couldn't go back, *or ahead*. You'll go

razy, he thought; there couldn't be any one answer to

1at.

He smoked the cigar down to the end and tossed it

way. It described a fiery parabola and fell hissing into the

vater at the edge of the sand. Cuban music and the

2und of off-key singing came from the *Dragoon,* and he

aw now that they'd turned on the spreader lights. With

1at radio and the lights and refrigerator they would run

1e batteries down. Then he was conscious of annoyance

vith himself. You've lived alone too long, he thought;

2u're beginning to sound like Granny Grunt. You form a

1ule-headed prejudice against a woman merely because

obody's ever told her you don't set highball glasses on

harts, and now while you're living one hour at a time on

1e wrong end of a burning fuse you're stewing about the

rain on a set of batteries. You ought to be playing

heckers in the park.

The pillow and the folded blanket were beside him. He

icked up the blanket and gave it a flipping motion to

pread it, and heard something drop lightly on the sand.

pparently whatever it was had been rolled up inside; he

aned forward and felt around with his hands, wondering

lly what it could be. He failed to find it, however, and

fter another futile sweep of his arms he flicked on the

igar lighter and saw it, just beyond the end of the blan-

et. It was a black plastic container of some kind, apparently a soap dish from a toilet kit or travel case. Well, at least he'd be able to wash up in the morning. He retrieved it, and was about to set it on the crates behind him when he heard a faint metallic click inside. He pulled the lid off and flicked on the lighter again. There were several things in it—none of them soap.

The first item was a money clip shaped like a dollar sign and containing several folded bills, the outer one of which appeared to be a twenty. The next was a small hypodermic syringe, its needle wrapped in cotton, and finally there was a tablespoon with its handle bent downward at right angles near the end, apparently so it would fit into the box. The rest of the space was taken up with eight or ten tightly folded pieces of paper. The lighter went out then. He spun the wheel again and set it upright on the sand beside him while he unfolded one of the papers. It contained just what he'd expected to find, a small amount of white powder, like confectioner's sugar. The lighter went out, and he sat frowning thoughtfully at the darkness.

He'd never seen any of the paraphernalia before, but had read enough about it to know what it was. There was a drug addict aboard. But which one? Didn't the police always examine the arms of suspected junkies, looking for punctures? He'd seen both of them with their shirts off and would have noticed if they'd had any; they didn't. But wait. . . . Obviously, the blanket must have come from one of the unused bunks. So it must belong either to Ives or to old Tango. And the odds were against its being Tango's. He probably couldn't afford a vice as expensive as heroin; all he had was a small disability pension from the First World War and whatever Mrs. Osborne paid him for living aboard the *Dragoon*. So it must be Ives'. She'd never said he was an addict, but then she'd never said much of anything about him. Well, it was a relief to know it wasn't either of the two still aboard; that's all they needed now, a wild-eyed and unpredictable hop-head to contend with.

He put the lid back on the box, scooped out a hole in the sand, and buried it. He'd better get some sleep so he could wake up around two or three a.m. By that time the should be sleeping soundly; he didn't have much hope he could get aboard the schooner without waking one of them, but he had to try. And if he got out there and found he couldn't get up the bobstay, he wanted to be sure of having an incoming tide so he could make it back.

Just as he was dropping off, he was struck by a curious thought. Why would Ives have a money clip? There at the Eden Roc Hotel, he'd taken his business card from a wallet when he introduced himself. Well, maybe he carried both. . . .

He opened his eyes. It was still night, and for a few seconds he was uncertain what the sound was that had roused him. Then he heard it again, and grunted with disgust; it was a feminine voice raised in maudlin song. God, were they still at it? He flicked on the lighter and looked at his watch. It was a quarter of two. Then he became aware the voice wasn't coming from the schooner; it was much nearer. He knuckled sleep from his eyes and sat up.

The night was still dead calm and velvety dark except for the gleam of uncounted tropical stars, and the blanket and his clothes were wet with dew. *"Come to me, my melan-choly ba-a-a-a-by,"* the voice wailed, not over fifty yards away now, and he heard the splash of oars. How in the name of God had she got hold of the raft? He walked down to the edge of the water just as it took form in the darkness, and could make out two people in it. When it grounded in the shallows, the man who was rowing got out. The figure was too slender to be that of Morrison. Ruiz ought to take out a card in the Inland Boatmen's Union, he thought.

"—for you know, dear, that I'm in love with youuuuuu!" Rae Osborne lurched as she stepped out, and Ruiz had to catch her arm to prevent her falling. He marched her ashore, pulling the raft behind him, and halted just in front of Ingram.

"I have brought you this one," he said in Spanish.

"Thank you a thousand times," Ingram replied, thinking sourly of *The Ransom of Red Chief.*

"Let us hope you have already had sufficient sleep, and that you are not a great lover of music."

83

Rae Osborne pulled away from him and weaved drunk enly toward Ingram. "Well, whaya know? M'rooned on desert island. With ol' Cap Ingram, the Ricky Nelson of the Garden Club. Hi, Cap!"

Ruiz turned away in unspoken contempt and disappeared into the darkness, towing the raft. Ingram took her arm and led her to the blanket and set her down with her back against the crates. In the moment before she started singing again, he heard oars going away in the night.

He noticed she still had her purse, and was pawing through it for something. Then the caterwauling trailed off, and she hiccuped. "Gol light, Cap?"

He knelt and fired up the lighter. She looked as if she'd had a large evening. The tawny hair was rumpled, she had a black eye that was swollen almost shut, and there was a purplish bruise on her left forearm. The bottoms of the white calypso pants were wet, of course, from wading ashore, and one leg of them had been ripped up the seam for several inches above the knee.

"I'm sorry," he said. He ignited the cigarette she had in the corner of her mouth, and put the lighter back in his pocket. *But not too sorry; you asked for it, sister.*

"Talk about survival training," she said with wry amusement. "I think that's about the nearest I ever came to being checked out on actual rape."

He muttered a startled exclamation and clicked on the lighter again. This time he had sense enough to look at the other eye, and he saw the cool, green glint of humor in it just before she winked. She was no drunker than he was.

8

"Is he gone?" she asked.

"Should be about halfway back."

"No wind that blew dismayed her crew, or troubled the Captain's miiiiiinnnnd!" she howled. Then she went on quietly, "He woke up while I was trying to get the raft overboard. I started singing again, and said I was going over to the yacht club to see if the bar was still open. I think I fooled him. Anyway, he'd apparently had it as far as the Bahamas Nightingale was concerned, so he brought me over here instead of tying me up."

"You can kick me now," Ingram said, "or wait till daylight if it's more convenient. I thought it was on the level."

"If you mean you thought I was drunk, you were pretty close to being right. Even with what I managed to ditch, I still had to put away a lot of rum; that Morrison must have been weaned on it."

"You were after the raft?"

"Principally. I thought we might be able to make it ashore somewhere. But I also wanted to get down in those cabins and see if I could find any of Patrick Ives' things."

"You were taking a long chance."

"It wasn't quite that bad. They wouldn't gang up on me; Ruiz isn't that type of thug. I wasn't sure whether I could handle Morrison or not, but it was worth the risk. After all, Ingram, I'm not Rebecca of Sunnybrook Farm. I'm thirty-four, and I've been married twice. If I lost the bet, I'd still survive."

"Did Morrison finally pass out?"

"Yes. Around midnight, I think. By that time I'd used up all the other routines, and didn't know any judo, so I pretended to be sick and locked myself in the biffy. I beg your pardon, what's the word?"

85

Ingram grinned in the darkness. "The head."

"The head. Anyway, when he quieted down, I came out, and he was asleep in the cockpit. But I wasn't sure about Ruiz. When he came back from over here and pulled the raft up on deck, he took some bedding and went up forward, so I couldn't tell whether he was asleep or not. I pretended to pass out on the other side of the cockpit and waited for over half an hour. Then I tiptoed up to where I could see him, and found he was asleep all right. I went below then, and started through the cabins."

"Did you find what you were looking for?"

"No. It wasn't a real thorough search, because I was afraid to take very long or turn on too many lights, but I found three suitcases and went through them and there wasn't anything that would identify Patrick Ives. Two of them belonged to Morrison and Ruiz, because their wallets were in them, but the third one—in one of those staterooms where the ammunition is—didn't have anything except the usual clothing and shaving gear and so on. It could be his clothing—that is, I think it would fit him— but for some reason they must have thrown his wallet overboard."

"Unless it was in his dungarees," Ingram said. "I mean, there in the dinghy. Those two men in the *Dorado* could have taken it.

"I thought of that, but somehow I don't think they did. I talked to them, remember?"

"Do you have any idea why they'd destroy his identification?"

"Just a minute," she said. "It won't do to get too quiet too suddenly. So duck." Her voice soared to a maudlin wail. *"Oh, when Irish eyes are smiling, sure 'tis like a morrrnnn in sprinnnngggggg—"* She chopped off suddenly, and said with amusement, "He'll think I fell down, or you threw something at me."

"It doesn't matter now whether he thinks you're drunk or not," Ingram pointed out.

"But it does," she said. She took a puff on her cigarette the tip glowed, revealing for an instant the handsome face with its prodigious shiner. There was something undeniably raffish about it, and appealing, and as attractive as sin. Must be atavistic, he thought; the view just before the clinch, after a Stone Age courtship.

"What are you driving at?" he asked.

"I don't want Ruiz to figure out I might have fooled him. He has a great deal of contempt for me, and I want to keep it alive."

"Why?"

"I think our only chance is for one of us to surprise him while Morrison's over here on the sand bar, and you're never going to get behind him if you live to be a hundred. I watched him all day, and that boy's cool."

"Also too tough to be knocked off his feet by a woman," Ingram said. "If he looks easy, it's just because you're seeing him alongside Morrison."

"It wouldn't have to be for more than three or four seconds, if we timed it right. However, we'll table that for the moment, and get back to Patrick Ives. It doesn't add up. He was aboard. They say he drowned."

"Are you *sure* he was aboard?" Ingram asked quietly.

"Positive. I managed to get Morrison talking about him a little tonight. Hollister was Patrick Ives, and nobody else. He never actually told Morrison that was his name, but he practically admitted it wasn't Hollister. And of course Morrison knew that Hollister-Dykes Laboratories thing was a lot of moonshine. He told Morrison he was an M.D. who'd got a bum deal from the ethics committee of some county medical association over a questionable abortion. That's pure Ives."

"Just a minute," Ingram said. "Was he a drug addict?"

"You mean narcotics?" she asked, puzzled.

"Heroin."

"No. He was a lot of other things, but not that."

"Are you sure?"

"Yes, of course. Unless he's acquired the habit in the past four months, at the age of thirty-six, which would seem a little doubtful."

"All right, one more question. Are you absolutely sure he was an aerial navigator during the war?"

"Yes."

"You're not just taking his word for it? I gather he was quite a liar."

87

"He was, but this is from personal knowledge. I knew him during the war, when he was taking flight training. He didn't make pilot, but he got his commission as a navigator and was assigned to a B-17 crew in England."

Ingram took out one of his remaining two cigars and lighted it. The pieces were beginning to fit together now, and he was pretty sure he knew why Ruiz was going over the hill. A little shiver ran up his back, and he hunched his shoulders against the darkness behind him. He told her about Ruiz' visit.

"Those boys are running from something really bad. I should have figured it out in the beginning, from the way Morrison acted. He'd rather risk anything than go back to Florida. But it was hard to see because as far as we know they hadn't killed anybody, and hadn't planned to. In fact, they'd gone to considerable trouble to get old Tango out of the way without hurting him—"

Rae Osborne broke in. "But somewhere along the line they did kill somebody."

"They must have."

"Patrick Ives," she said excitedly. "Why didn't we see it before? The body was here near the *Dragoon,* but the dinghy was picked up over twenty miles away, in deep water."

"That's perfectly natural," Ingram pointed out. "The body was submerged—and probably on the bottom—a good part of the time, so it was acted on only by the tides. But the dinghy was carried off to the westward by the wind and the sea."

"Yes, but look, Captain— Don't you see? That's the reason Morrison wouldn't let anybody go out and get his body when Avery saw it from the plane and called us on the radio. We'd find out Ives hadn't drowned at all, that he'd been killed."

"No," Ingram said. "If Morrison had had five years to work on it, he couldn't have dreamed up a story that matched the evidence as perfectly as that did. I was already pretty sure the man had drowned, even before I got aboard the *Dragoon,* and I don't have any doubt at all it happened exactly the way Morrison said it did. What he didn't want us to find out was that the man wasn't Ives."

"What?"

"I don't think Ives was even aboard when they left Florida."

"But he had to be. The watch—"

"This other man, whoever he was, must have been wearing the watch. That's all. I don't know whether Ives *is* the one who's been murdered, but somebody was, and it happened ashore where it can be proved, not out here where it could be covered up as an accidental drowning. Naturally, Morrison wasn't going to tell us about it as long as he had a perfectly good ready-made explanation for Ives' being missing. He was going to have his hands full as it was, forcing me to take them down there and watching us so we didn't escape. If we knew the real story, we'd jump overboard and try to swim back to Miami."

"He intends to kill us, then, when we get to this Bahía San Felipe?"

"I think so. And Ruiz can't quite hold still for anything as cold-blooded as that, so he's about made up his mind to pull out. If he can."

"I see," she said. She was silent for a moment, and then she asked, "You're absolutely certain there was another man?"

"There has to be." He scooped up the black plastic box and showed her the contents, and told her about the compass.

"That's the reason they got in here over the Bank and ran aground. They've been lost. Remember, they stole the *Dragoon* on Monday night, so it couldn't have been any later than Wednesday night when they loaded the guns down in the Keys, and sailed. This isn't over a day's run from anywhere in the Keys, because even if it'd been calm they would have used the engine, but they didn't go aground here until *Saturday* night. So for at least two days they've been wandering around like blind men because the compass is completely butched up by all that steel—those gun barrels. Even if one of them knew how to use the radio direction finder well enough to get a fix by cross-bearings, it's no good unless you've got a compass. Here's what happens—say they get a fix from the RDF, figure

89

out the compass course to where they want to go, and then after a while they check their position again, and find out they've gone at maybe right angles to where they thought they were heading. So obviously the first position must have been wrong. Or was it the second position? D that about three times, and you're so hopelessly lost you wouldn't bet you're in the right ocean."

"But," she said, "didn't Ruiz say they knew about th steel's effect? And that Ives had checked the error befor they left?"

"Sure," Ingram replied. "On one heading. That's wha gave it away—I mean, that he'd already disappeared ever before they sailed. It couldn't have been Ives who did that He'd have known better. Admittedly, he could have go pretty rusty in fifteen years, and the compasses on thos planes were probably gyros, but nobody who'd ever stud ied navigation could know that little about magnetic com passes. They're basic, like the circulation of the blood t the study of medicine. And you don't adjust one by find ing out what the error is on one heading and the applying that same correction all the way around. It different in every quadrant, so you have to check it i every quadrant. Actually, on some headings, what the were doing was multiplying the error instead of correctin it."

"Then I guess there's no doubt," she said. "But i somebody's been killed, why do you suppose the polic didn't say anything about it?"

"They don't always tell you everything they know. An maybe they don't know, or don't have any reason yet t connect it with the theft of the *Dragoon*."

"Yes, that's possible." She flipped her cigarette away i the darkness. "If we could surprise Ruiz and get that gu away from him while Morrison's over here, could we mak it ashore in the raft?"

"Not to Florida. With luck we might get back acros the Bank to Andros, but I don't know whether we'd mak it across the island. However, with Ruiz off our backs an Morrison stuck over here, I think I could refloat th schooner. At least, we could get on the phone and call fo help."

"Morrison might get back aboard, if it took very long."

"No. He couldn't swim it with a gun."

"Would that thing he carries around with him shoot from here to the boat?"

"I think it'll probably carry that far, but it wouldn't be very accurate. However, there's another angle on that. Once we start bringing those cases of ammunition over, he could use these rifles. We wouldn't be able to move on deck except at night. But there's something I wanted to ask you. You say Ruiz was sleeping on deck—that wouldn't be way forward, would it?"

"Yes. Right in the bow. Why?"

He nodded grimly. "I thought so. Before we spin any more gossamer dreams about what we're going to do after we fool Ruiz, we'd better take up the question of *how*."

"What do you mean?"

He told her about the idea of swimming out and trying to get up the bobstay. "He saw that was the only place I could possibly get aboard. So I'd have to step right over him. Dripping wet."

"I know it won't be easy," she agreed. "As I said, I watched him all day, and he never once let me get behind him while you were alongside with the raft. But maybe he will now that I'm just a stupid drunk, and obviously harmless."

"I can't let you do it," Ingram protested. "Ruiz is no punk hoodlum. He's tough all the way through, and he's got reflexes like a cat."

"Let's don't waste time worrying about me. I'll be behind him, and I don't think he'd shoot me, anyway. It's you we've got to think about. If he breaks loose and gets that gun before you reach him, he'll kill you, so unless you're sure you can make it, don't try. But we've got to have a signal. How about this? I'll be calling you Herman, and referring to him as Pancho—you know, endearing myself to everybody—but when you hear the name Oliver, get ready to come aboard."

"All right." They had to try for it sometime, and the sooner the better. It *had* to be when Morrison was out of the way. He looked at the blur of her face just before him in the soft tropic night. "I owe you an apology," he said.

91

"Why?"

"For what I thought."

"Oh, really?" she said indifferently. It was clear she didn't care what he thought. "If you'll excuse me, I think I'll wander off to the other end of our little sandpile and see if I can get some sleep."

"No," he said, getting up abruptly. "You stay here and use the blanket and pillow." Ignoring her protests, he strode off in the night. Fifty yards away he stretched out on the sand with his head pillowed on an arm and stared up at the black infinity of space while he finished his cigar. He felt like a pompous and overweening fool who'd just been thoroughly deflated, and he was certain she'd done it deliberately. Well, there was no law said you had to stick your neck out and get it stepped on. He threw away the cigar and surrendered himself to the weariness that assailed him. When he awoke, her face was just above him in the gray beginning of dawn, and she was shaking his shoulder. The blanket was spread over him. He threw it aside and sat up, grinding a hand across his face.

"I think you had a nightmare," she said. "I heard you cry out, and you were trembling as if you were cold, so I put the blanket over you. Then you began to beat at the ground with your hands."

"It was just a bad dream," he said.

"Oh-oh. Somebody's coming from the boat."

He turned his head and saw the raft approaching across the flat, dark mirror of the sea. "Remember the signal," she said softly.

"Oliver. But be sure you're behind him."

"I will be. Good luck." She turned away and went over to pick up her purse by the stack of crated rifles, and was combing her hair when Ruiz grounded the raft in the shallows and motioned to her. Ingram watched her wade out, a bedraggled but indomitable blonde girl with a black eye and torn calypso pants, and heard the brassy idiocy of her greeting. "Hi, Pancho. I feel like hell, I theeeenk. And if I ever catch the lousy parrot that slept in my mouth . . ." They moved off toward the *Dragoon*.

Ingram stood up, pushing his leg straight against the stiffened tendons and aware of the soreness in every muscle of his body. You're too old and beat-up for this kind of duty, he told himself. He wondered why she had put the blanket over him, but dismissed the speculation as futile; he'd never figure her out. Walking out into the water, he scooped up some and scrubbed his face, and noted professionally that the tide appeared to be at a standstill. It was slack high water. Ruiz came back with the raft. He got in and pulled out toward the *Dragoon*, and as they came alongside he studied her critically. She was still hard and fast aground, not even completely upright yet. Solid-looking wooden boxes with metal straps were lined up along the port rail and stacked in the cockpit. She was gray and ghostlike in the dim light of early morning, and everything was saturated with dew. Morrison stood on the crates in the cockpit, the inevitable BAR slung in his arm and an expression of driving impatience on his face. It was clear he was in an ugly mood. "How about it?" he asked, as Ingram stepped aboard.

"A long way to go yet," Ingram said.

"All right, here's the ammo. Twenty-five boxes of it, round two hundred pounds to a box. Ruiz and I carried it up while you were flaked out over there on your fat with Mama-san. Probably have to take 'em over one at time. Ruiz'll put a rope on 'em and help lower 'em into the raft so you don't drop any."

"Do we get anything to eat?" Ingram asked.

"There's a mug of coffee and some Spam. That's all anybody's going to get till this boat's unloaded."

Rae Osborne was seated aft by the binnacle smoking a cigarette. "How about breaking out the rum?" she asked sulkily. "I think I've got crabgrass on my teeth."

Morrison whirled on her. "You lay off the sauce or we'll tie you up. We got enough to do without dodging some drunk staggering around in the way. You can have some coffee."

She sniffed. "Coffee! Big deal."

"And you better remember to stay clear of Ruiz. He's fussy about people coming up behind him, and he'll bend our teeth."

"Ruiz and what other wet-back? Don't forget I own this

93

boat, little man. And I could buy you in sets, for book ends."

Ruiz stared through and beyond her without any expression at all. Morrison grunted contemptuously, and turned away. She was doing fine, Ingram thought, as he sipped his coffee; then he remembered the night in Nassau and wondered just how much of it was acting. She baffled him. He got permission to visit the head, with Ruiz following him with the Colt, and then rowed Morrison over to the sand spit. The labor began. When he came alongside each time, Ruiz had one of the boxes balanced at the edge of the deck with a line around it and would stand back in the cockpit to lower away while Ingram settled it onto the bottom of the raft. They were brutally heavy for their size, and he wondered if they would move all of them before the fabric bottom gave way. At the other end, however, Morrison hoisted them to his shoulder seemingly without effort and strode across the flat toward dry ground. The sun rose, and grew hot. The tide began to ebb. And still Ruiz' guard was impregnable.

Ingram could see Rae Osborne moving about the after deck apparently at will when he was away from the schooner, but the moment he came alongside Ruiz motioned her astern and away from him. She cajoled, whined, threatened, and grew abusive, trying to get a drink, and all of it availed her nothing. A light breeze sprang up from the southeast around nine a.m., but in half an hour it died away and the heat grew unbearable as the sun attacked them from all directions, reflected from a sea as smooth as polished steel. They stopped for an hour and a half during the peak of the ebb, but were back at it by eleven. By 12:30 the tide had passed low slack and was beginning to flood again. They had unloaded sixteen of the boxes of ammunition, a little over a ton and a half. And still she'd had no chance at Ruiz. They had the rum put away where she couldn't find it, and feigning drunkenness was obviously out of the question.

On the next trip, however, he caught a change in the pattern. Maybe she had solved it. She was below when he

94

came alongside, and didn't return to the deck until after he was loaded and pulling away. She moved listlessly, as though she were ill. He delivered the box to Morrison and rowed back. This time she sat quietly in the after end of the cockpit until the loading operation was completed and he was clear of the schooner's side. Then she arose, slightly doubled over, and hurried toward the ladder.

"Again?" Ruiz asked.

"So you must have bad water on here," she snapped.

Ruiz shrugged. "Water? How would you know?" But she was gone down the ladder.

All right, Ingram thought: I read you loud and clear. But it probably wouldn't be the next trip; she'd build it up more subtly than that. The next did go by without incident. It was after one now, and the flood was quickening. When he came alongside on the return, butterflies moved softly inside his stomach; one mistake, or one tiny lag in reaction time, and he might be dead within the next few minutes. She was seated on the deck with her feet on the cockpit cushions, aft on the opposite side. He gave her only a passing glance and caught the lifeline stanchion. The box of ammunition was balanced on the edge of the deck just level with his shoulder, and Ruiz had hold of the line.

She leaned forward slightly. "Don't stand between me and that ladder, Oliver."

Ruiz gave her an indifferent glance as she stood up. Ingram reached for the box, walked it over the edge of the scupper, and let Ruiz take the strain on the line just as she started up the deck beyond him. He saw her turn and fall, and at the precise instant she landed on Ruiz' shoulders he gave a savage yank on the line. The two of them fell forward onto the cushions on the low side of the cockpit; just in front of him. The box of ammunition struck the edge of the raft and almost capsized it as it plummeted into the water. He had hold of the lifeline and was lunging upward then, throwing a turn of the raft's painter around the lifeline as he went over it into the deck. Ruiz had pushed to his feet, but Rae Osborne was still fast to his back with her arms locked around his waist and over the flat slab of the automatic. The Latin clawed at her hands, broke her grip, and pulled the gun free of the tangle and slammed back against the cushion on the starboard side as the two men went down locked together in the bottom of the cockpit. Ingram could feel the hard weight of the gun between their bodies, and got a hand around the muzzle.

Not a word had been uttered, and there was no sound except the sibilant scrape of canvas shoes against the deck, and the meaty impacts of flesh against flesh and of furious bodies against wood, and the tortured gasps of breathing. Ruiz was incredibly strong for a man of his slender build, but not strong enough. Ingram got the other hand around his wrist, locked it in a paralyzing grip, and slowly forced the gun to his right until it was out from between their bodies. He twisted savagely at the muzzle and tore it from Ruiz' grasp. Pushing back, he sat up with his back against the binnacle, switched the gun end in his hand, and leveled it at Ruiz' face as he fought for breath. He clicked off the safety, which Ruiz had never had a chance to do.

"Go below," he said to Rae Osborne. "Bring up some of that line they used for lashings."

She went down the ladder. Ruiz sat up and slid backward, his eyes never leaving the gun. It was intensely silent for a moment as they both came to rest, and Ingram was conscious for the first time that there had been no firing from Morrison. He must have seen it. Then it occurred to him that with the *Dragoon*'s port list and their sitting in the cockpit they were out of sight now, and even if the big man had had time to go back and pick up the BAR he was too much the pro to shoot when there was nothing to shoot at.

"When you come back," he called to Rae Osborne, "don't stand up. Crawl back to where I am."

"Right, Skipper. I've got some rope now."

Ruiz said softly, "You're not going to tie me up."

Ingram centered the gun on his chest. "But I am, *amigo.*"

"I won't go back. Go ahead and shoot."

"Who'd you kill?"

Ruiz made no reply.

"Was it Ives?"

Ruiz still said nothing.

"Where did you hide the tubes you took out of the radiophone?"

"We threw them over the side," Ruiz said.

Rae Osborne's face appeared then in the companion hatch and she crawled out into the cockpit with the line in her hand. "Don't move," Ingram warned Ruiz as she slid past him. I'll have to beat him up before I can tie him, he thought, and looked forward to it with distaste. But it was the only way; she couldn't hold him still with the gun. He wouldn't pay any attention to it.

Rae Osborne handed him the line and started to turn to face Ruiz. Then she gasped, and cried out, "The raft!"

Ingram's eyes shifted to the left. The painter was gone from the wire lifeline. At the same instant, Ruiz leaped to his feet, got one foot up on deck, and dived over the starboard side, all in one continuous motion. Ingram cursed and sprang up. He could see him under the water, swimming straight out from the schooner. The raft was some thirty or forty yards away, being carried eastward on the flooding tide. It was easy to see what had happened. Either his own lunge when he'd come aboard or the impact of the falling case of ammunition had propelled it aft far enough for the tide to carry it under the stern, and the single turn he'd been able to take with the painter hadn't held it. He tracked Ruiz with the gun. He was coming up now, less than fifteen yards away.

His head broke the surface. He shook water from his face and opened his eyes, and for a fraction of a second that seemed like an hour to Ingram they looked squarely at each other across the sights of the gun. Ingram tried to pull the trigger. Then he sighed gently and let his arm drop. Ruiz turned and began to swim, not even bothering to dive again. He knew I couldn't do it, Ingram thought. Rae Osborne was beside him now, and she cried out, "We can't let him get it!"

Bitterly, without speaking, Ingram held out the gun to her. She pushed it away, and said, "No, I mean shoot the raft."

He raised the gun, and shot, but he was low. The

bullet made a little splash six or eight feet short of the raft. He raised the muzzle slightly, but before he could fire again, two small geysers erupted in the water just under them and something slammed into the deckhouse off to their left with a shower of splinters. "Down!" Ingram snapped. They dropped back into the cockpit. The professional combat team was in action now; Morrison was covering Ruiz with the BAR.

Ingram raised his head to peer over the edge of the deck. The raft was at least seventy-five yards away now; the chances of his hitting anything at that distance with a handgun were too dim to justify wasting the ammunition. A couple of holes wouldn't disable it, anyway; they'd find a way to plug them. He looked to the left, and could see Morrison. He was about two hundred yards away, wading out on the flat south and west of the sand spit to get as near the schooner as possible and to try to intercept the raft if Ruiz failed to catch it. Ingram estimated the line of its drift and saw he wasn't going to make it unless he dropped the gun and swam; the water was nearly up to his chest now, and was growing deeper. Hope flared for a moment, and then died. It didn't matter; Ruiz was over hauling it.

Morrison was ignoring them now that Ruiz no longer needed cover. They stood up and watched bitterly as the latter caught the raft and pulled himself aboard. Beyond him, Morrison brandished the BAR above his head in jubilation.

"Do you suppose they'll try to come aboard right now?" Rae asked.

"I don't know," Ingram said. "They might wait till dark if they know for sure we can't get the telephone working . . ." His voice trailed off then as he stared out at the raft. Ruiz had picked up the oars, but he wasn't pulling toward Morrison. He was headed due south, away from both the schooner and the sand spit.

"What is it?" Rae Osborne asked, puzzled. "Where's he going?"

"Over the hill," Ingram said softly. He shook his head. A hundred miles—with no compass, and no water.

Morrison was plunging ahead, beckoning violently with

is arm. Then he stopped and leveled the BAR. Ruiz kept right on rowing. They saw the burst chew up the surface behind him and come upward across the raft, and then his body shook and jumped under the impact and he fell sideways and rolled over with his head and shoulders in the water. The collapsing raft spun slowly around in spreading pink and drifted away to the eastward on the tide. Rae Osborne made a retching sound and turned away.

9

Morrison had turned and was wading back to the sand pit.

Rae Osborne sank down unsteadily on the cockpit cushions. "Why do you suppose he did it? Ruiz, I mean."

Ingram shook his head. "Whatever his reasons were, he took 'em with him. I think he'd finally just had all of this thing he could stomach. He wasn't Morrison's type of goon."

"I think Morrison's a psychopath."

"Ruiz was probably beginning to have the same idea."

"At least Morrison didn't get the raft. But how will losing it affect us?"

"Not a great deal," Ingram replied. "I was going to use to carry out the kedge anchor, but I can still swing it. We'd better get started, though. It'll be high tide in around three hours."

"But what about the radio?"

"We'll try that first. But don't bet on it."

They went down the ladder. The air was stifling below decks, with a sodden and lifeless heat that seemed to press in on them with almost physical weight. There were still some thirty or forty wooden cases stacked along the sides of the large after cabin, and the deck was littered

with discarded rope lashings. He turned to the radiotele
phone on its shelf aft on the port side. He loosened th
knurled thumbscrews and slid out the drawer containin
the transmitter section. Four of the tubes were gone fror
the sockets. Rae Osborne looked at him questioningly.

"Ruiz told me they threw them overboard," Ingrar
said. "He could have been lying, of course, but I'm nc
so sure. They wouldn't have let you wander around o
here so freely if there'd been any chance of getting thi
thing operating again."

"That's right, too. But at least we can try."

He nodded. "And another thing. While you're searching
keep an eye open for a diving mask. I could use one, an
most boats have a few kicking around somewhere. Yo
start up in the crew's quarters and work back through th
galley. I'll start here and go forward. But first I'd bette
check Morrison."

There was a pair of big 7-x-50 glasses in a bracke
above the navigator's table on the starboard side. H
grabbed these and went on deck. Crouching in the cock
pit, he focused them on the sand spit. At first he couldn
see the man, and began to feel uneasy. Then he swept th
area around the piled boxes again and caught a momen
tary glimpse of the broad back just behind them. He wa
bent over, working on something on the ground. Ingra
nodded. Trying to chew his way into those boxes, h
thought; he's got six hundred rifles over there and enoug
ammunition for two or three small wars. He'll try his be:
to keep us pinned down here till he can make it bac
aboard.

He returned below and began the search for the tube:
He went over every inch of the after cabin, moving th
crated guns around to get at things. He searched th
drawers, the chart stowage, medicine locker, inside tl
RDF and the all-wave radio, book racks, clothing locker
and even in the bilge. He found a carton of radiotelephor
spare parts which contained several tubes, but they wei
apparently all for the receiver; at any rate, none matche
the type numbers stamped beside the empty sockets. F
moved into the two double staterooms that faced ea(
other across the narrow passageway connecting the ma

bin and the galley, but found nothing except the suit-
se which had apparently belonged to Ives.

By this time Rae Osborne had been through everything
the galley. "No tubes," she said. "But here's a diving
ask I found in a locker up forward." They went aft. In-
am looked at his watch; it was 2:20 p.m.

"Scratch the radiotelephone," he said. "So we either
float the schooner or stay here."

"Can we do it?" she asked.

"I think so—" He broke off suddenly and listened. She
d heard it too, and looked at him with some alarm. It
as a rifle shot, coming to them faintly across the water.
here was another. She waited tensely, and then shook
r head with a rueful smile. "Makes me nervous, wait-
g for it to hit."

"Don't give it a thought," he said. "If it's going to hit
ything, it already has before you hear the shot. The bul-
t travels about twice as fast as the sound. I think he's
ghting in one of those rifles. Keep listening."

He had hardly finished speaking when something struck
e hull just forward of them with a sharp *thaaack,* fol-
wed a fraction of a second later by the sound of the
ot. She nodded.

There were four or five more shots, and then the firing
ased. "He's warning us to stay off the deck, so we can't
anything about getting her afloat," Ingram explained.

She looked worried. "What do we have to do? And *can*
e do it?"

"I think so. The first thing is to finish lightening ship.
I need the mattresses off all those bunks."

She gave him a burlesque salute, and a lopsided smile
at was inhibited on one side by the grandfather of all
iners. "One order of mattresses coming up. I wouldn't
now what for, but you seem to know what you're doing."

He grinned briefly. "Let's just hope you still think so
venty-four hours from now."

While she was bringing the mattresses, he picked out
ree of the long wooden boxes that apparently contained
sassembled machine guns, and shoved them up the lad-
r. After going into the cockpit himself but staying down
keep out of sight, he laboriously worked them up onto

the deck and lined them up end-to-end along the starboard side of the cockpit. When he was putting the secon
one in place, Morrison began shooting again. Two bulle
struck the hull, one directly below him. She was pushin
the mattresses up the ladder now. There were ten alto
gether. He propped six up along the outside of th
machine-gun boxes and laid four in a pile atop the dec
house just forward of the hatch. They should shield th
cockpit against direct gunfire and the danger of flyin
splinters. They knelt for a moment behind them, restir
in the shade of the awning. "Cozy," she said appre
ciatively. Just then Morrison opened fire again with
string of three shots. All three of them struck the sam
spot, the outer mattress propped against the forwar
machine-gun box.

Ingram frowned. "With iron sights, at three hundre
yards? He's bragging." Two more slapped against th
same mattress; they could see the upper edge kick as the
hit. He grabbed the glasses and peered cautiously over th
ones atop the deckhouse. Morrison was firing from
prone position, using a rest made up of one of the case
and what appeared to be a rolled blanket, the one they
left over there. But it was the rifle that caught his eye ar
caused him to whistle softly; it had a telescopic sight.

"What is it?" she asked.

"Scope-sighted deal," he explained. "Apparently son
of those were either sniper's rifles or sporting guns."

"That's bad, I take it?"

"Not particularly, but I'd have been just as happy wi
something a little less specialized." He was thinking
having to take that kedge anchor out; it was beginning
look considerably less simple. Morrison could shoot, ar
he had something to shoot with.

She looked at him curiously. "You sound like anoth
gun expert. Were you one of those jungle command
too?"

He shook his head. "I was in the Navy. I never shot
rifle during the whole war, except in boot camp. But
used to do a lot of hunting."

"Where?"

"Texas, and Sonora, when I was a boy."

"Where are you from?"

"Corpus Christi. My father was a bar pilot there."

She looked around musingly. "You don't suppose this might set a new record of some sort for the places Texans run into each other?"

"I doubt it. But I'd better get to work."

"What can I do?" she asked.

"Nothing at the moment. Just stay back and keep down." He went below and began shoving the heavy wooden cases up the ladder. When he had several in the cockpit, he came up, lifted them onto the deck on the port side, and shoved them overboard. There was something very satisfying in the splash they made; he was sick to death of Morrison and his damned guns. It was a long, hard job, and he was winded and drenched with sweat as he took a last look around the cabin where nothing remained now of its late cargo but the confused litter of rope. He went above and shoved the last ones overboard, and looked at his watch. It was 3:40. Glancing out across the water, he noted the incoming tide had slowed now; it should be slack high in a little over an hour. He wiped sweat from his face. "So much for that."

Rae Osborne indicated the five cases of ammunition still lined up along the port rail near the break of the deckhouse. "How about those?"

Ingram shook his head. "We keep them for the time being. They're our hole card, in case this other stuff doesn't work."

"I feel useless, letting you do everything."

"I'll have something for you in a minute. In the meantime, whenever Morrison gets quiet over there, check him with the glasses."

"You think he might try to swim out?"

"I don't think he will in daylight, but we can't take any chances. Keep your head low."

Ducking down the ladder again, he went forward to the locker beyond the crew's quarters and dug out an anchor. It was a standard type, with a ten-foot section of heavy chain shackled to the ring; it would do nicely. He carried it aft and came back for a heavy coil of nylon anchor warp. While he was getting this out, he came

103

across a pair of four-sheave blocks and a coil of smaller line he could use for a tackle. He grunted with satisfaction; it would be better than the main sheet to haul with. Trying to use the *Dragoon*'s anchor windlass up there on the exposed foredeck would be sheer suicide. Morrison would have a clear shot at him with that scope-sighted rifle. He carried it all aft and dumped it in the cockpit. At the same time Morrison cut loose with a string of four shots as if he were practicing rapid fire. One of them struck the side of the mainmast and ricocheted with the whine of an angry and lethal insect.

Rae Osborne watched with rapt interest as he wedged the anchor's stock and bent the nylon warp to the ring at the end of the chain. "Where does it go?" she asked.

He nodded astern. "Straight aft as far as I can get it."

"But how do you take it out there?"

"Walk and carry it."

She grinned. "So you ask a silly question—"

"No, that's right. I'll admit it's not quite the standard procedure, but it's about all we've got left. That's what I wanted the diving mask for."

"But how about breathing?"

"That's easy. The water's not over seven or eight feet deep until I hit the channel, and then it's not over twelve."

"What about Morrison and that rifle?"

"No problem," he said, wishing he felt as confident about it as he was trying to sound. He lowered the anchor over the side and arranged the coil of line in the bottom of the cockpit. "You pay it out. And when you get within twenty or thirty feet of the end, hang on."

She nodded. "Roger."

He took the automatic out of his belt and put it on the seat beside her. "You know how to operate the safety on this?"

"No. I don't know anything about guns at all."

He showed her. "That's all there is to it, besides pulling the trigger. If Morrison should make it out here and get aboard, kill him. None of this TV routine of pointing at him and trying to impress him. Put it in the middle of his chest and empty the clip."

She looked apprehensive. "I think I get the message."

104

ll this is just in case you don't come back? Is this anchor eally necessary?"

"Absolutely. But there's no danger. I'm just covering ll bases."

"All right. Anything else?"

"That's all, except looking the other way till I get in the ater."

She turned away while he stripped down to his shorts nd dropped over the side with the mask. Adjusting the tter, he went under. Some of the boxes he had thrown verboard were piled up almost to the surface under the chooner's side. He pulled them down so the schooner ouldn't fall over against them on the next low tide in e event they didn't get off this time. There was no hull amage, at least on this side. Her keel was stuck in the ottom—just how far, he couldn't be sure. A lot would epend on what kind of tide they got this time. He sur- ced for another breath, and Rae Osborne was leaning cross the deck looking down at him. "Be careful," she id. He nodded, went under, and picked up the anchor.

It was still heavy, even submerged, but the weight held is feet firmly against the bottom so he had no difficulty alking. He noted with satisfaction that the water was ightly deeper astern; once they got her back as far as velve or fifteen feet, they'd have it made. He walked ent over and leaning forward to cut down the water's sistance. He turned and looked back. The water was as ansparent as air; he was going straight, and the line was aying out beautifully. He was about thirty feet past the ern now. Dropping the anchor, but holding a bight of e line in his hand, he let himself rise until his face roke the surface, took a quick breath, and pulled down gainst the weight of the anchor and its chain. He picked up and went on.

The bottom so far was all sand, with patches of grass. here were numbers of conchs scattered about in the ass, and once he saw a leopard ray and a small bar- cuda. The current was beginning to bother him now as e got more line out. The schooner was fading out behind m, and it was harder to keep in a straight line. He rfaced again. Nothing happened. Morrison still hadn't

seen him. The bottom sloped downward. He was goir
down into the channel, in water ten to twelve feet deep
Just before the schooner disappeared completely behin
him, he picked out an isolated clump of grass ahead fc
a landmark. The going was harder now; it was backbreal
ing work pulling the line. He surfaced again, and just a
he sucked in his breath and went under, something ex
ploded against the water off to his left like the slap of
canoe paddle. He felt a little chill of apprehension. Mor
rison had located him at last.

The next time he surfaced, the explosion was neare
and the third time he barely had his head under when th
bullet struck and ricocheted off the surface so close t
him he could feel the impact in the water. Nobody coul
sight and shoot that fast; Morrison was tracking him. H
had his course figured out, and how far he was going eac
time, and was waiting. Well, he could solve that. H
picked up the anchor, but this time, instead of plowir
on until he was out of breath, he stopped after three step
and began pulling the line toward him and gathering it i
coils. When he surfaced, he was twenty feet short c
where Morrison was expecting him. When he went dow
again he was able to make a fast thirty feet with the coile
slack line he had. Both times, the shots were wide.

But he was beginning to be afraid now. He wasn
getting enough oxygen for the tremendous exertion c
pulling that anchor warp across the tide, and carbo
dioxide was accumulating to dangerous levels in his bod
Those hurried gulps of air weren't enough; he had to sta
longer on the surface, or drown. Then, suddenly, he cou
get no slack at all. He'd come out to the end. He too
another breath, heard the bullet strike somewhere beyor
him, and worked the anchor back and forth, digging
fluke into the bottom. He started back, going very fa
now, pulling himself hand over hand along the war
When he came up for air, Morrison wasn't expecting hi
in this direction, and there was no shot. He had to surfa
once more on the way back, and then he could see t
schooner's stern ahead of him. Just as he was about
black out completely he came up under her side and l

n the surface too weak to move as he held onto the line
nd drank in air in long, shuddering breaths.

Rae Osborne was just above him, the fear still showing
n her face. "Let's don't go through that again. I thought
e was going to kill you."

Ingram could only nod. It was two or three minutes be-
ore his strength began to return. "Toss the line up over
ie boom," he directed, "and pass me the other end." He
aught the doubled line and managed to pull himself on
eck. She disappeared down the ladder while he slipped
n the khaki trousers, and when she came back she silent-
 handed him a towel. He collapsed on the cockpit seat
nd mopped at the water running out of his hair.

"That was a little too much," he gasped. "I guess I'm
a old man."

"Not old, Ingram. But a man."

He glanced up quickly. There was sudden confusion in
er face. "Well, thank you," he said, surprised.

The old arrogance of manner was back now and every-
ing was under control. "Forget it," she said indifferently.

"Sure. But sometimes I wish I could figure you out."

"Really? I thought you'd done a beautiful job of
at—*and* expressing your opinion."

"So I was wrong," he said uncomfortably. "But I did
y to apologize, didn't I, when I found out it was just an
t?"

"Oh, that." She dismissed it with a shrug. "I was talk-
g about Nassau, there in the Carlton House bar."

He stared at her, completely baffled. "Carlton House?
Then were you in there?"

It was her turn to stare. She sank down on the opposite
de of the cockpit just as one of Morrison's 30-caliber
ugs struck the foremast and went screaming off across
e water; neither of them even noticed it. "Oh, good
ord! You mean you didn't even see me?"

"No," he replied. "I didn't see you anywhere. Except
ere in your room."

"Ouch! Don't remind me of that. I guess I'm the one
ho owes you an apology. But I was furious. I thought
ou'd done it deliberately."

"I'm sorry," Ingram said. "That's happened to me before. I'm an absent-minded goof at times, and I think was reliving my past." He was conscious of still bein puzzled, however; she was too intelligent to get very upse over anything as petty as that.

She grinned. "I don't think you've grasped the rea beauty of it yet. Most of the time I seem to have all th social grace of a water buffalo. It's just carelessness, bu it can lead to some very embarrassing situations. You re member I got out of the taxi to go shopping, and aske you to take my things on to the hotel and register for me I was two blocks away before it dawned on me this wa a little on the casual side, to say the least, since I didn know anything about you at all. There was no tellin what you might think, or how you might take it. And t make it worse, I couldn't even remember exactly what I' said. But of course when I got out to the Pilot House Clu everything was all right. Apparently whatever I'd sai hadn't been *that* ambiguous, and I'd been embarrasse about nothing. It even struck me as a little funny—unt I walked into the Carlton House bar where you wer drinking beer and sat down around the curve of the ba and smiled at you, and you looked right through me an three feet out the other side. So much for the amusin little situation."

"I *am* sorry," Ingram said. "I don't know what to say

"Maybe under the circumstances, we'd better just g back and start over." She solemnly held out her han "I'm Snafu Osborne, the girl with two left feet and stranded yacht."

"Cousin Weak-eyes Yokum, ma'am," he said gravel and took her hand. "And I'll get your boat back in t water if you'll promise never to tell anybody I looked you and didn't see you. They might lock me up."

She laughed. "Well, I'm glad we've got that straigh ened out. Now what's next on the schedule?"

"All we have to do now is get a tackle on that anch warp. You can help me reeve these blocks." He slipp the T-shirt over his head and put his sneakers and t watch back on. After laying the two blocks out in o posite ends of the cockpit, he began reeving the li through the sheaves. When it was completed, he crawl rward along the port side of the deckhouse and made ne end of the tackle fast to a cleat. Then he led the nchor warp in through the chock on the stern, hauled it s tight as possible by hand, and took a purchase on it ith the tackle. He hauled again. With the multiplying verage of the big four-sheave blocks the anchor warp ame out of the water astern, dripping and as tight as a rumhead. The blocks were overhauling now. He stopped ne warp off at a cleat on the stern, ran the tackle out gain, took a new purchase, and hauled. The anchor was olding beautifully, and the warp ran straight out now, s rigid as a steel bar. He took a turn around a cleat to old the strain, and looked forward along the deck. The *ragoon* was on an even keel as well as he could tell, nd the tide was still flooding almost imperceptibly onto ne Bank. They might make it, he thought; they just ight. He held up crossed fingers. She smiled as they ced each other crouched on the bottom of the cockpit.

"What do we do now?" she asked.

"Just hold what we've got. In a few minutes we'll start ne engine and try to back her off."

"And if she doesn't come off?"

"We'll try again on the next tide. In the morning."

"I'm sorry I got you into this mess, Ingram."

"You didn't," he said. "Ives did."

"I'm still responsible. You just got caught in the line f fire."

"Who was Ives?" he asked.

"My first husband," she said.

"Oh." He turned and looked out across the water. That was the reason you didn't tell the police?"

"No. I didn't tell them because I still wasn't sure then at Hollister was Patrick Ives. I wanted to find out defitely. There wasn't much they could do, anyway, as long the boat was out here."

"And you were afraid something had happened to m?"

"No." She smiled faintly. "I was trying to catch up with m for the same reason you were. I have a stubborn reak in me, and I hate being played for a sucker. To be

quite frank, he made an awful fool of me. Did Ruiz sa
anything at all while I was down there getting the rope?

"No. Except that I'd have to go ahead and shoot. H
wouldn't go back. I asked him if it was Ives they kille
but he wouldn't say."

"Do you think it was?"

"It could have been," Ingram said. "It's a cinch som
thing happened to him between the night they stole th
boat and the night they loaded the guns aboard."

A bullet slammed into the hull just forward of the
followed immediately by the sound of the rifle. Mayb
Morrison was trying to drive them crazy. He looked o
at the surface of the water that was almost at a standst
now as the tide reached its peak. Reaching past her,
switched on the ignition, set the choke, and pressed th
starter. On the second attempt, the engine rumbled in
life. He let it warm up for two or three minutes an
checked the wheel to be sure it was amidships.

Their eyes met. He nodded. "Here we go. We hope

He put the engine in reverse and advanced the thrott
Bracing his feet against the end of the cockpit, he caug
the tackle and hauled. Rae Osborne slid over beside hi
and threw her weight on the line. There was vibratio
from the engine, and water rushed forward along the sid
of the schooner from the churning propeller, but th
Dragoon remained hard and fast against the bottom wi
the unmoving solidity of a rock.

Thirty minutes later he cut the ignition and slump
down in the cockpit, exhausted. As the sound of th
engine died, a bullet slammed into the furled mains
above them. There was something mocking about it,
thought; maybe it was Morrison's way of laughing
them.

10

ae Osborne tried to look cheerful. "Well, there's always morrow. Do you think the tide might be higher then?"

"It's possible," Ingram said. "But not necessary. We'll et her off then. I'm going to haul her down on her side."

"How?" she asked. "And what does that do?"

"It tilts the keel out of a vertical plane, so she doesn't ed so much water to float. That's why I saved those oxes of ammunition. We'll sling them on the end of the ain boom and swing it out over the side for leverage. e'll have to wait till after dark to rig it, though, so he n't pick us off with that rifle."

"Then there's nothing that has to be done now?"

He shook his head. "Why?"

She smiled. "At the moment, the thing that'd do more r my morale than anything else in the world is a bath. think Morrison said they filled the fresh-water tanks—"

"Go ahead," he said. "Use all you want. We may have pump some of it overboard, anyway."

"Wonderful." She started to scuttle toward the ladder, t paused, her face suddenly thoughtful. "You don't ppose any of those bullets are going through the hull? lon't know why, but there seems to be something inde- nt about being shot at in the shower."

He grinned. "Not at three hundred yards, and from the gle he's shooting. They're just gouging splinters out of e planking."

She went below. He picked up the glasses and peered utiously over the top of the deckhouse. Morrison was ll lying behind his rest, smoking a cigarette while he sually reloaded the rifle. He's got no food, Ingram ught, but he does have water; he could last for several ys. But obviously he had to get back aboard; he might able to swim that far, but not carrying a rifle or the

111

BAR. However, if he managed to empty enough of those cases and could nail them together, he might make a raft of sorts on which to carry the gun. At any rate, he wouldn't try it until dark, knowing they had Ruiz' automatic. They'd have to stand watch all night.

He located the rod and sounded the two fuel tanks. As nearly as he could tell, the starboard one was still full and the port a little less than half. They had about two hundred gallons aboard. The fresh-water tanks were forward where he couldn't reach them, but if they were even half full, they had at least that much water. Getting rid of some of it would help. The water could be pumped overboard, but there was no way to ditch the gasoline unless he could find a hose and siphon it out. He could, of course, start the engine and let it run, but the amount it would use up wouldn't justify the noise. He disliked engines, anyway, and having to listen to them always irritated him. He went below and ransacked all the lockers but could find no hose except a few short pieces that had been split for use as chafing gear. He heard the shower stop and knocked on the door.

"Yes?" she called out.

"Just let it run and empty the gravity tank," he said. That would help, and he could pump some more overboard later. He found a coil of new nylon line, gathered up an armload of the rope lashings, and went back to the cockpit to size up the job before it grew dark.

The topping lift probably wouldn't hold it alone, not half ton out there on the end of the boom; but if he backed it up with the main halyard and reinforced the halyard fall with this heavier line it should be safe enough. The awning would have to come down. He'd have to memorize the location of everything; it wasn't going to be easy, having to do it all in the dark, by feel. He looked at his watch; it was a little after six now, and the tide was beginning to ebb off the Bank. A timber creaked as the *Dragoon* settled a little and began her slow, inevitable list to port. He began cutting the rope lashings to make slings for the ammunition boxes. A cat's-paw of breeze blew out of the south, ruffling the awning and making it cooler for a few minutes. The sun was low in the west.

Rae Osborne came up the ladder. She looked cooler and much refreshed in spite of the fact that she had no other clothes to change into; her hair was neatly combed now, and her mouth made up. He looked at the handsome face with its spectacular shiner, and grinned. "You look wonderful."

She touched the puffed eye with her finger tips, and smiled ruefully. "It's a mess, isn't it?"

"Well, as shiners go, there's certainly nothing second-rate about it. It seems to match your personality, somehow."

"You mean beat-up?"

"No. Colorful. Flamboyant. And undefeated."

She laughed. "I'd better think about that. I'm not sure but what it sounds like some biddy in a barroom brawl."

She went below again and returned after a while with a plate of tuna sandwiches and a pitcher of water. They sat facing each other across the bottom of the cockpit while daylight died in a drunken orgy of color and the intermittent sound of Morrison's gunfire. She gazed westward to the towering and flame-tipped escarpments of cloud beyond the Santaren Channel, and mused, "I know it sounds stupid under the circumstances, but I'm beginning to see what makes people crazy about the sea. It's beautiful, isn't it?"

"You've never been around boats before?" Ingram asked.

"No. My husband just took the *Dragoon* in on a business deal; neither of us had ever owned a boat of any kind, or even wanted to. He planned to sell it to get his money out of it, but he died just a few weeks afterward—almost a year ago now. He was killed in the crash of a light plane he and another man were flying out to Lubbock to look at a cattle ranch."

"What business was he in?" Ingram asked.

"Real estate." She smiled softly. "Or that's one way of putting it. Actually he was a speculator. A plunger. It's a funny thing—he was the gentlest person I've ever known and he looked like an absent-minded math teacher in some terribly proper school for young girls, but he was one of the coldest-nerved and most fantastic gamblers

113

you ever saw in your life. He was forty-eight when I
was killed, and he'd already made and lost two or thre
fortunes. Actually, it never made a great deal of di
ference to me. Beyond a point, piling up money you dor
need seems like a waste of time, especially if you ha
no children to spend it on or leave it to, and most of t
time I wasn't even sure whether we were rich or in del
He was away from home so much I had a business of n
own, just to have something to do. I never was any goc
at that social routine. I'd worked most of my life, an
women from better backgrounds and expensive schoc
always made me feel inferior, and I'd get defensive an
arrogant and make a fool of myself. I've always be
crazy about sports cars, so I had a Porsche agency,
little showroom in a shopping center near where we live
I still have it."

"Why were you so long trying to sell the *Dragoon?*"
asked.

"I couldn't sell it. There was a tax lien on it. Wh
Chris was killed, several deals he had pending fell throug
and it developed he was overextended again and pre
shaky financially. On top of that, he'd just got an adve
ruling on an income-tax thing, so the government fro
everything until it was paid. I didn't want it sold
auction at a big loss, so I held on and the lawyers fina
got it straightened out after about eight months. The
wasn't a great deal left other than the schooner and
house. Anyway, as soon as it was cleared up—I think
was in March—I came over to Miami to see some ya
brokers about selling her, and that's when I ran i
Patrick Ives. For the first time in thirteen years." F
voice trailed off, and she stared moodily out across
water.

"That's when he went aboard?" Ingram asked.

"Yes. Maybe I'd better tell you about him. It's not v
flattering, but since between the two of us we seem
have dragged you into this, you're entitled to an exp
nation. I first met him in 1943 when he was an Army
Force cadet at an airfield near the little town I ca
from. He was from Washington—the state, I mean.
were practically in flames over each other right from

114

first, and he wanted me to marry him before he went overseas. I would have, too, except that I still lacked a few months of being eighteen, and my parents put a stop to it. We carried on a torrid correspondence all the time he was in England, and did get married when he was reassigned to an airfield in Louisiana just before the end of the war. When he was discharged, he decided to go back to school. He wanted to study medicine. He'd already had two years at the University of Washington, before he went in the service. So we moved to Seattle. I got a job, and he tried to start over where he'd left off two years before. It just didn't work out. Maybe we were both too immature, I don't know. But that quonset-hut, GI-Bill, all work-and-no-play type of college life, with another six long years of it staring us in the face before he could even hope to graduate from medical school, was just too much for us. We fought a lot, and he began to fail in all his subjects." She fell silent for a moment. Then she made a weary gesture, and went on. "We split up. I came back to Texas, and we were divorced that summer —1946. I never saw him again, or even heard of him, until the afternoon four months ago when I was flying to Miami to see about selling the *Dragoon*. He boarded the plane in New Orleans, and took the seat next to mine.

"Those things when you're very young are apt to be pretty intense, but no bitterness lasts for thirteen years, and after the first shock wore off it was more like a meeting of old friends than anything. It took us all the way to Tampa to get caught up. I told him what I was going to Miami for, and I'll have to admit it didn't lose anything in the way I said it: I was running over to see about disposing of my late husband's yacht. That was a little childish for a woman almost thirty-five years old, but for some reason I seemed to think I had to impress him—maybe because he was so obviously successful himself. But anyway, that's probably when he began to form the picture of the wealthy widow.

"He told me about himself. He'd got his M.D. from the University of California medical school and had quite an extensive surgical practice in the San Francisco hospitals—specializing in chest and heart surgery. He was also connected with the medical school as a part-time lecturer on surgical techniques, which brought him to the subject of this trip he was on. It seemed he and some scientist from Cal Tech had worked out a new and more simplified type of heart-lung machine for use in operations where the heart had to be by-passed. I didn't understand any of it, of course, but it sounded very impressive to me. He was demonstrating it at a series of operations that had been scheduled at a number of medical schools. He'd just been at Tulane, and he was on his way to Miami, and he was as tickled as a young boy when he learned I was living in Houston, because he was going to be in Galveston in another week or so, at the University of Texas medical school.

"You've met him. You know what he's like. He's a very handsome man with a world of drive and charm, and frankly I was flattered by all the attention he gave me. He took me out for dinner and dancing both nights I was in Miami, and rented a car to drive me down to Key West to look at the *Dragoon*. We were aboard her most of one afternoon. He gave me a lot of advice about what price to hold out for, and said he had a thirty-five-foot yawl of his own on San Francisco Bay. I knew he had sailed small boats on Puget Sound when he was a boy. He was very sharp with Tango for not keeping the cabins and the decks cleaner, and they got in an argument, which is probably the reason he was sure Tango would remember him if he saw him again.

"Well, to cut a long and humiliating story down to a short and humiliating story, about a week after I got home he showed up in Houston. He was busy down in Galveston during the day, of course, but he took me out somewhere every night, and told me a lot more about himself. He was a lonely and unhappy man. He said he'd been married again but it hadn't worked out, and he was divorced now. Of course, by this time I'd dispelled the myth of the wealthy widow, but still one of the most infuriating parts of the whole thing was the precise way he sized up just *exactly* how much he could take me for. Seven thousand, five hundred dollars. Any more and I

116

might have balked because I couldn't afford it. Any less and it might not have been worth all his trouble. Apparently he must have spent his days appraising everything I owned, like a professional weight-guesser.

"The actual mechanics of the swindle were simple enough. He and the Cal Tech scientist were forming a small company to produce around a hundred of the heart-lung machines already contracted for by hospitals all over the country, and one of the original five stockholders had dropped out. And while there was no question that the company would make a great deal of money, the main thing was to be careful about letting control fall into the hands of sordid businessmen who might try to cut corners and cheapen the machine. So for the sake of having the odd share in the hands of somebody with sympathy and understanding, *and* for old times' sake . . . You can take it from there. I gave him a check for seventy-five hundred dollars. After two days went by without any word from him, I called the dean's office at the medical school, and of course they'd never heard of anybody named Patrick Ives. I hired a private detective agency to find out if there was any truth in anything he said. There wasn't. He was wanted in several places on the Coast and in the Middle West for cashing worthless checks, always posing as a doctor. This was probably the first time he'd used his real name for years, and then only to me. And when the Miami police told me about that watch found in the *Dragoon*'s dinghy I had a feeling it must be his."

Ingram nodded. "And you thought if you could catch up with him you might get some of the money back?"

"No. It was four months ago, and the way he lives he'd have spent it all by now. I just wanted to try to get the schooner back to salvage *something* out of the mess. I'd been kicked where it hurt—right in the pride—and I was pretty bitter about it. I think I even took some of it out on you, that first night. When you said you weren't going to charge me anything for helping me find her, I didn't believe you, frankly. I thought you had an angle too. Great little judge of character, this Osborne girl."

"Well, you couldn't be blamed too much for believing

117

him," he said. "After all, he wasn't a thief when you knew him before."

"Don't be so modest, Ingram. I was talking about how wrong I was about you."

"Apparently there was an epidemic of it that night. I was wrong too. In fact, I was convinced I wasn't going to like you, so I may have set a new record for being mistaken."

Her face was a pale blur across from him in the thickening dusk. "Thanks, Skipper."

He came alert then, suddenly aware it had been twenty minutes or more since they'd heard a shot from Morrison. Goofing off, he chided himself; they could get themselves killed. "We'd better get on the ball," he said. "There are two ways Morrison can get aboard now—up the bobstay under the bowsprit, or up this anchor warp. Either way, though, he'll make enough noise so we can hear him if we're listening. I'll be working back here, so you go forward. Lie down on the port side of the forward deckhouse and just listen. If you hear anything at all, sing out."

"Right." She disappeared into the darkness forward.

He sat still for a moment. The vast silence was unbroken except for another creak as the schooner lay over a little farther on the outgoing tide. He stood up and began taking down the awning. He rolled it up, deposited it on the deckhouse out of the way, and freed the main boom from its supporting gallows. The mainsail was jibheaded, so there was only one halyard; he unshackled it from the head of the sail, bent a piece of line to it, and hauled down on the fall at the base of the mast until he could reach the wire. He made the new nylon line fast at the thimble, hauled down on the other end again, carried it aft, and shackled it to the end of the boom. He also made two pieces of light line fast to the end of the boom for use as guys, since he was going to need the main sheet to hoist the ammunition boxes. He freed the lower end of the sheet.

After raising the boom with the topping lift until it was well clear of the gallows, he secured it, and hauled on the halyard until—as well as he could tell in the dark by

118

eel—the strain was evenly divided between the two. This was important, because if either one had to take the load by itself it might part, in which case the other would carry away too. He swung the boom over a little to port to get it away from the gallows, and secured it with the guys. He stopped then to listen, and to put a hand on the tackle holding the anchor warp. There was only silence, and no vibration of any kind on the line. "You all right?" he called out softly in the darkness.

"Just fine, Skipper," her answer came back.

The worst of it, he thought, was that there was no way to guess what Morrison would do, or what he might be planning out there in the dark. He was dangerous, and would be as long as he was alive and anywhere near. Even if there were no longer any hope of escape, he'd still kill them if he got the chance, just as pointlessly as he had killed Ruiz for trying to cross him. The shots at his head while he was taking out the kedge anchor proved that; if Morrison couldn't escape, nobody was going to.

He muscled the five boxes of ammunition aft along the deck until they were under the outer end of the boom. Locating the rope slings he had cut, he put one about each box with a double wrap, crossing at right angles, and tied it off with a free end about eight feet long. He shackled the lower block of the main sheet to the sling where it crossed and hoisted away until the blocks were jammed and would go no farther, caught the free end of the sling, and made it fast about the boom and the furled sail several feet inboard from the end so as to have room to suspend all five of them. Then he slacked off with the tackle, and disengaged it. The second box went up, and the third. He stopped to listen for Morrison, and then cautiously hoisted the fourth. He was working right under the boom, and if anything carried away now he'd be crushed. Before he hoisted the fifth, he stood on it and reached up to push a hand against the twin wires of the topping lift and the halyard. It was all right; they appeared to be taking an equal strain. He hoisted the fifth box. Everything held. He sighed with relief and gently hauled the boom outboard just enough to suspend the boxes over the water a few feet off the port quarter. If it gave way now, at least they wouldn't come crashing down on deck. He tied off the guy and secured the main sheet again to hold it in position. Ducking down into the cockpit he flicked on the cigarette lighter and looked at his watch. It was 9:35. Low tide in about two hours, he thought; the deck was listing sharply to port now.

He slipped forward along the port side and knelt beside her. She sat up. "We're all set," he said. "Nothing to do now until high tide."

"That'll be about dawn, won't it?"

"Right around there."

"Do you think we'll make it then?"

"Yes," he said quietly. "We'll get off this time. But why don't you go back to the cockpit and get some sleep? I'll watch for Morrison."

"You can't watch both places at once."

"Yes. I can sit here where I can keep a hand on this tackle holding the anchor warp. If he tries to climb it, I'll feel the vibration."

"I'd rather stay up and talk," she said. "We *can* talk, can't we?"

"Sure. As long as we keep a lookout."

They slid aft until they were beside the cleat holding the tackle, and sat down on the sloping deck with their backs against the deckhouse in the velvet night overlaid with the shining dust of stars. There was no breath of air stirring, and no sound anywhere, and they seemed to be caught up and suspended in some vast and cosmic hush outside of time and lost in space. They sat shoulder to shoulder, unspeaking, with Ingram's left hand resting lightly on the taut and motionless nylon leading aft, and when he put the other hand down on deck it was on hers and she turned hers slightly so they met and clasped together. After a long time she stirred and said in a small voice, "This is a great conversation, isn't it? I hope I didn't promise anything brilliant." He turned and looked at the soft gleam of tawny hair and the pale shape of her face in the starlight and then she was in his arms and he was holding her hungrily and almost roughly as he kissed her. There was a wild and wonderful sweetness about it with her arms tight around his neck and the strange, miraculous breach

120

ng of the walls of loneliness behind which he had lived so long, and then she was pushing back with her hands against his shoulders.

"I think maybe we *had* better talk," she said shakily.

"I expect you're right," he agreed. "But you'd better get started."

"Two platoons of Morrisons in full pack and dragging a jeep could walk right over us and we wouldn't even notice it." She took a hurried breath, and went on. "And as to whether Morrison is the only hazard, I admit nothing. I plead the Fifth Amendment. But what do they *do* to these damn stars down here, anyway? Polish them? Now it's your turn to say something, Ingram. You can't expect me to carry on a conversation all by myself."

"I think you're magnificent," he said. "Does that help?"

"Not a bit, and you know it. As a matter of fact, it can't be much of a secret that I think you're pretty wonderful yourself, but at least I told you so under perfectly ordinary, everyday circumstances, in bright sunlight with a man shooting at me with a rifle. I didn't pull a sneaky trick like silhouetting my big square head against a bunch of cheap, flashy stars that anybody can see are phony. . . ." Her voice trailed off in a helpless gurgle of laughter, and he said, "Oh, I'm not making any sense. Why don't I just shut up?"

When he raised his lips from hers she drew a finger tip along the side of his face and said softly, "You never have to hit Ingram twice with a cue. Not ol' Cap Ingram. Do you think I'm pretty horrible?"

"Hmmm. No-o. That's not the *exact* word I'd use."

"I am, though. I'm as brazen as a Chinese gong and about as subtle as a mine cave-in. I've been sitting here for twenty minutes wondering when in Heaven's name you were going to accept the fact you had to kiss me. All escape was cut off, and there was no honorable way to retreat."

He touched his lips gently to the puffed and battered eye. "Shut up," he said.

"The only thing I didn't realize was how fast it might start to get out of control. I should have, though. I worked so hard at trying to loathe you I was worn out to begin

121

with. Did anybody ever tell you you're a hard man to detest, Ingram? I mean, at a party or something, where there was one of those pauses in the conversation when everybody's trying to think of something to say—"

She gasped as a bullet struck something above their heads and screamed off into the night. On the heels of it came the whiplash sound of the gun from somewhere directly behind them. They slid down and lay flat on deck against the side of the house. The rifle cracked three more times in rapid succession, two of the bullets striking the hull on the other side. She lay pressed against him; he could feel her trembling.

"I'm scared," she whispered. "It's gone on too long."

"We'll be away from here in the morning. And we're perfectly safe down here."

"You don't think we ought to go back to the cockpit?"

"No. This is fine. We've got so much list now he couldn't hit us if we were sitting up." He was thinking of those boxes of ammunition suspended back there and wondering what would happen if they were hit. They probably wouldn't explode, but some of the cartridges might fire. There were five evenly spaced shots then. Two of them struck the schooner's hull.

"He's nearer, isn't he?" she asked.

"Yes. The tide's gone out, so he's waded out on the flat south of the sand spit."

"How close can he get?"

"Not under a hundred and fifty yards. That channel is still over his head, even at dead low tide." I wonder how he's carrying the ammunition, he thought. Probably made a pack of some sort out of the blanket.

"How can he see to shoot in the dark?"

"He can't, very well. You'll notice he's missing a lot. But he's right down on the surface, firing at the silhouette, and he probably has something white on the muzzle of the rifle. Maybe a strip of his shirt."

Another bullet struck the hull. Two apparently missed. Another hit. Subconsciously, he was counting. They would probably go through the planking from where he was firing now, and with the list the schooner had some of them would be below the water line, which was probably wha

Morrison had in mind. It wouldn't matter, though, unless there were a great number of them; she had two bilge pumps, one power-driven, and could handle a lot of water.

"I'm tired of being shot at," she said. "And sick to death of being so stinking brave about it. I want to have hysterics, like anybody else."

He held her in his arms and spoke against her ear. "Go ahead."

"It was mostly just blackmail. But keep talking there."

"Do you know when it first dawned on me that I was probably crazy about you? It was when Ruiz came after you this morning, and I watched you wade out to the raft, torn pants, black eye—"

"Well, it figures, Ingram. Who could resist a vision like that?"

"No." He groped for words to express what he had actually seen, the crazy honesty of her, the insouciance, the lithe and unquenchable spirit. "You were so—so damned *undefeated.*"

"Let's don't talk about me. I want to hear about you."

The firing went on. They talked. He told her about Frances, and about the *Canción,* and Mexico, and the boat-yard in San Juan. He mentioned the fire only briefly but she sensed there was more to it, and drew the rest of the story from him.

"That's why you limp sometimes, isn't it?" she asked quietly. "And what you were dreaming about when you were beating at the sand."

"Yes," he said.

"Ingram, I'm sorry."

"It's all right now."

The schooner's list increased as the tide approached dead low, and it was difficult clinging to the sloping deck. The shooting stopped for fifteen or twenty minutes, and then started again. He had to go back after more ammunition, Ingram thought. If he's going to swim out here, he'll do it on the flood so if he doesn't get aboard he can make it back. He wouldn't tackle it on the ebb because he might get carried out to sea. Flicking on the lighter for an instant, he looked at his watch. It was a few minutes past midnight. The tide should have turned already. There was another

shot. I'd better go below and check now, he thought, whil
I'm still sure where he is. He told her.

"You think water's coming in?" she asked.

"Maybe a little. If there is, we'll pump it out."

"You won't be long?"

"No."

"If anything happens to you—"

He kissed her. "What could happen?" He crawled af
and dropped into the cockpit just as Morrison shot agair
Somewhere in the blackness below there was the sound o
running water. That didn't make sense. It couldn't *run* ir
not that way. He started down the crazily slanting ladde
and even before his head came below the level of the hatc
he smelled it, and the old nightmare of terror reached u
to engulf him. He lost his grip on the handrail and fel
and wound up against the port bulkhead under the radio
telephone, on his hands and knees in the cold lake of gaso
line that extended up out of the bilge as the boat lay ove
on her side. He could hear it still running out of the punc
tured tanks in the darkness behind him as he fought agains
the whisperings of panic. If he lost his head completel
and ran into something the fumes might kill him before h
could get out. He pushed off the bulkhead and reache
upward, groping for the ladder. His fingers brushed i
Then he was up in the cockpit, stretched out on the cush
ions on the port side, shaking all over and trying to kee
from being sick. His hands and his legs from the knee
down were very cool from the evaporation of the gasoline

11

He thought of her, and hoped she hadn't heard him com
up. He needed a few minutes alone to pull himself to
gether; he couldn't face her this way. But still he was go
ing to have to tell her; there was no way to avoid i

heir chances of escape were almost gone now, and until
e got the last of that gasoline out of there they were
ving on a potential bomb. A pint of gasoline in the
ilge could form an explosive mixture in the air inside a
oat, and they had two hundred gallons of it. Just one
ark from anything—static electricity, a light switch,
ven a short circuit in the electrical system from one of
Iorrison's bullets—and the *Dragoon* would go up like
Roman candle.

Using the engine was out of the question. Even if any
el remained in the tanks when the schooner righted her-
lf, trying to start it would be an act of madness when
e slightest spark at the starter brushes or the generator
uld blow them out of the water. And even after he
imped the bilges dry, it wouldn't be safe; not for days.
hey had to be washed out, and ventilated. But the mere
nsideration of these technical matters was beginning to
ve its calming effect; potentially ghastly as they might
, they were still technical, and fear receded as the pro-
ssional mind took over. They didn't need the damned
gine to get back to Florida, if they could only get her
loat. And there was still a chance of that—a slight one,
t a chance. Pumping the gasoline out would lighten her
another thousand to fifteen hundred pounds, and they
ight be able to pull her off with the kedge alone now
at he had the gear rigged to haul her down on her side.
t that moment another bullet slapped into the hull up
rward and the sound of Morrison's rifle came to him
ross the water. That completed the job. He had hated
w people in his life, but right now he hated Morrison,
d he thought of him with a cold and implacable anger.
iey wouldn't be defeated by him. If it's the last thing I
er do on earth, he thought, I'm going to beat him.

He slipped forward along the deck. When he knelt be-
le her, she said, "I smell gasoline."

"It's on me, a little on my trousers." He told her about
She took it well, as he should have known she would.
don't think it's going to change things too much. We
ay still get off on this tide. Just remember, don't smoke.
n't turn on a light. Don't even go below. And that
eans even after I get it pumped overboard."

"I understand. What shall I do?"

The schooner creaked as she came up a little in th
darkness. "Just listen for Morrison," he said. "As long a
he's shooting, it's all right, but the tide's flooding now an
it'll drive him off that flat pretty soon. If he's going to tr
to get aboard it'll be within the next few hours. Go rig]
up to the corner of the forward deckhouse so you'll b
sure to hear him. The gasoline going overboard will mak
some noise."

"Right, Skipper."

"You're magnificent. Or did I tell you that?"

"You can be as repetitious as you want. I don't min
at all. Actually, I'm scared green. You just can't see it."

He took her face between his hands. "I'm going to g
us out of here."

"Have I ever doubted it?" she asked. "You might ca
me a fan. I've been watching you in operation for th
past—good Lord, has it only been two days?"

"All I've done so far is lose."

"That could be a matter of opinion, Ingram. But, liste
—if you expect me to keep my mind on Morrison, we'r
going to have to spread out."

She disappeared into the darkness forward. He wer
back to the cockpit. There was no way now to tell wh
time it was, but it must be after one. High tide would b
between 4:30 and 5:30; call it four hours from now. Usir
the power-driven bilge pump was out of the question nov
of course, since they couldn't start the engine, but th
hand pump would empty it easily in less than an hou
and still take care of any water that might seep in throug
Morrison's bullet holes. It was on the narrow bridge dec
between the cockpit and the break of the deckhouse. H
groped around until he found the plate that covered :
grabbed the handle, and began pumping. He could he
the gasoline going over the side in a satisfying strear
Off in the darkness to starboard Morrison's rifle cracke
but there was no sound of the bullet's striking the boa
Five minutes went by. The gasoline continued to flo
he'd have it out in a half hour, he thought, the w
it was going. Then the handle became harder to rais
and the sound of the stream died to a trickle. It stoppe

126

cursed, wearily and bitterly, sunk for a moment in
ter despair. Damn Tango and his filthy housekeeping.
here was no telling what kind of mare's nest of litter
ere was in the bilges.

The answer, of course, was simple enough; go down
ere, locate the suction, and clear it. He thought of it,
d shuddered—thought of the dead blackness so im-
netrable that directions ceased to have any meaning, of
eeling in gasoline and running his arms down in it
ile the flaming torch that was Barney Gifford did its
enzied and spasmodic dance along the perimeter of his
nd. He mopped sweat from his face. Well, she thinks
u're a grown man; either go down and do it, or go up
ere and tell her that she's wrong. It's all mental, any-
ay; as long as there's nothing to set it off, it's harmless,
ovided you come up for air before you breathe too
uch of it. He began taking off his clothes. He put the
n and his watch and sneakers on the seat beside them
he could find them in the darkness, and went down
e ladder clad only in his shorts.

At the bottom, he turned and faced aft, visualizing the
cation of the pump. The cabin sole was dry here, near
idships; the gasoline that had come out of the bilge
s out near the bulkhead as she lay over on her side.
e could hear it still running out of the tanks, but not as
ongly now. Kneeling, he groped around until he found
e access hatch, and lifted it out. He started to think of
rney, and the nightmare began to crowd in around the
ge of his mind. He pushed it back and concentrated
dly on the job. The fumes were choking him; it was
ne to go up for air. He went up the ladder until his
ad and shoulders were out of the hatch, breathed deeply
r two or three minutes, and returned. Locating the open-
g, he groped around in the gasoline beneath it, but
uldn't find the bilge pump suction. He stepped down
o it, in gasoline up to his knees, knelt down, and felt
rther aft. There it was. He could feel the soggy mass
papers around it. The fumes were beginning to make
n sick now. He pulled the papers out and threw them
ward the starboard side of the cabin. Then he became
are that there were more, both on the bottom under

127

his feet and floating free where he had stirred them
with his splashing around. He felt one brush against
hand, caught it, and lifted it out, and from its size a
shape he was pretty sure what it was. Somebody h
stored cans of food in the bilges without removing t
labels.

He swore softly in the darkness, and managed to fi
out three more. A bullet tore through the planking wi
a splintering sound and slapped into the bulkhead som
where just forward of him. He shuddered, thinking of t
electrical circuits, but went on groping. Then it occurr
to him that he was doing more harm than good. As lo
as they were lying on the bottom they probably would
get into the suction, but he was stirring up more than
was getting out. He climbed back to the cockpit, wip
the gasoline off his legs and arms with the towel, and b
gan pumping. In five minutes the suction was clogg
again.

He went down into the blackness and the fumes a
the border country of nightmare once more, and w
crouched knee-deep in gasoline with his face just abo
its surface when he froze suddenly and the skin along I
back drew tight with the stabbing of a thousand needl
It was a sound, the familiar, homelike throbbing of
electrical appliance nobody ever really listened to—t
refrigerator motor. He'd forgotten all about it until no
the thermostat had tripped, and it had come on. I
waited for the white and blinding flash of the explosic
Nothing happened. Seconds ticked away. His legs we
trembling, but he breathed again, softly, almost tentativ
ly, as though even daring to hope might tip the scal
the other way.

There was nothing he could do. He could go forwa
to the galley and disconnect it, but breaking the circ
while there was a load on it *would* cause a spark. No
of the switches or electrical fittings aboard were vapc
proof. He went on waiting. A full minute must have go
by now. Maybe the fumes weren't as dense up the
since the bulk of the gasoline was aft. Strength beg
to return to his legs and arms, and his mind cleared st
ficiently to warn him of the other and ever-present dang

asphyxiation. He hurriedly cleared the pump suction
1 went back up the ladder. The motor was still hum-
ng its industrious way along the edge of eternity.

He caught the pump handle, and for a second he was
scious of a crazy impulse to laugh and wondered if
d begun to crack. Even this simple act of pumping the
ff overboard could blow it up; the friction of the gas-
ne against the walls of the pipe and against the air
1 the water as it fell over the side into the sea generated
ugh static electricity to set it off. Except for the saving
ce of the almost saturated humidity around them,
y'd probably be dead already. He went on pumping.
er a while you get numb, he thought; you can't absorb
more, so it rolls off. This time it was nearly ten min-
s before the pump clogged. As the trickle died and
nce closed over the boat once more, he became aware
t the refrigerator motor had cut out. He went below,
ped his way forward, and pulled out the plug. He
ared the suction, and returned to the pump. In less
n two minutes it choked off again. He went below and
ared it. When he came back he vomited over the side
1 his skin was inflamed and itching from immersion
the gasoline. He pumped. It was scarcely twenty strokes
ore the stream died to a trickle and quit. He sat down
the cockpit seat.

It was hopeless. He was never going to pump it over-
ard until it was light down there and he could see those
ers and get them all out at once. Dipping the towel
r the side to wet it, he scrubbed at his legs and arms
an attempt to get some of the gasoline off them, and
: his clothes back on. The taste of defeat was bitter in
mouth and he wanted to smash his fists against the
k. Maybe they would never get the *Dragoon* off. They
re doomed to stay here forever—or until some random
rk blew them into flaming wreckage.

No! He stood up. They weren't whipped yet; there was
1 the fresh water. He slipped forward and knelt beside
e Osborne. "I may have got a third of it out," he
led, after he had told her about it. "Pumping some of
fresh water overboard will help too. We've still got a
nce."

"Of course we have. She's coming up all the time."

He'd been oblivious to the passage of time, and wo[n]dered how long they had now until high tide. "How lo[ng] has it been since there was a shot from Morrison? I forg[et] about him."

"Nearly a half hour."

That was ominous. He hated leaving her up here alo[ne] trying to watch both ends of the boat at once, but he h[ad] to get that water out. Every pound was important. Th[en] he had an idea. "Did you ever do any fishing?"

"Once or twice." She sounded puzzled. "Why?"

"That's what you're going to do right now." He we[nt] aft to the cockpit and groped around for a piece of li[ne] that was long enough. Making one end fast around t[he] anchor warp, he came forward, paying it out, and put [it] in her hand. "Pull it taut, and just hold it. If he gets [up] back there, you'll feel him."

"Fine. Where will you be?"

"In the galley. Just yell, and I'll be here in five se[c]onds."

He slipped down the forward hatch and felt his w[ay] back to the galley. The pump was over the sink. [He] groped around until he found several pots, filled the[m] with water, and set them aside for insurance. There w[as] no telling how much was in the tanks, and if he pump[ed] them dry before he realized it, they would be in troub[le.] He began pumping into the sink and letting it run ove[r]board. The gasoline fumes weren't as bad here as in t[he] after cabin, but they were still too strong to breathe f[or] very long. He opened the porthole above the sink a[nd] leaned forward to get his face in front of it. He was [all] right then. A timber creaked as the schooner righted he[r]self a little more on the rising tide. He wondered ho[w] much longer they had, and increased the tempo of [his] pumping. Sweat dripped from his face. If he could g[et] even a hundred gallons overboard it would lighten t[he] schooner by at least another eight hundred pounds. Th[en] it occurred to him that if many of Morrison's bullet hol[es] were below the water line as the tide came up and s[he] righted herself, salt water might be running into the bil[ge] faster than he was pumping out the fresh. Well, th[at]

130

s nothing he could do about it. Maybe it was hope-
s, and had been from the first. It was beginning to
em now that he had been aboard this grounded boat
ever, and he wondered if he would even recognize the
el of one that was afloat and free beneath his feet.

He heard her footsteps on deck, and then she spoke
ftly near the porthole. "Skipper?"

Morrison, he thought, and felt for the gun against his
omach. "Yes?"

"Everything's all right. I just wanted to tell you it's
tting pink in the east. I can see the water a little now,
d it seems to be hardly moving."

He hurried on deck. She was right. It was still too
rk to see the sand spit, but there was definitely a touch
color in the east. He strained his eyes outward toward
e surface of the water, and could make out that the tide
s flooding very slowly now. They'd be at the peak in
s than half an hour.

"Here we go," he said. "Keep your fingers crossed."

"Right. But is there anything I can do of a more prac-
al nature?"

"There will be, very shortly. Just wait here. It'll be
most an hour before he has light enough to use that
opesighted rifle, so I'm going to haul with the anchor
ndlass this time. We'll get this schooner off or pull her
two."

He hurried aft and gathered up the free end of the
rp. Then he returned to the bow, threw five or six
ns on the windlass drum, set the ratchet, and handed
r the end. "Just hang on," he said. He inserted the bar
one of the slots at the edge of the drum, and winched
upward. The warp came taut. Going aft again, he
cked the tackle and cast it off. The warp was clear the
l length of the deck except at the corner of the for-
rd deckhouse. It wasn't much of a fairlead, but it
uld have to do.

She was on an absolutely even keel, as nearly as he
uld tell. If she was ever going to come off, she should
it now. He wondered if he should dog down the ports
ng that side. No, it would take a lot more weight on
t boom than he had now to bring her down that far.

"Hang on," he called out to Rae Osborne. "We're goi~
to take a list."

"Okay, Skipper," she called back.

He slacked off the main sheet, and hauled on the gu~
The main boom with its dangling cluster of ammuniti~
boxes swung slowly outward. The deck began to list. T~
boom came up against the sheet and stopped. He ran ba~
and pulled some more slack through the blocks, a~
hauled the guy again. The boom came directly outboa~
and the deck rolled down until the scuppers were alm~
awash. Then he wanted to cry out with joy; there h~
been a definite tremor under his feet, the feeling of~
boat that was alive. She'd moved!

Rae Osborne called out excitedly. "I felt something!"

He laughed. "What you felt was a schooner trying~
see if it remembers how to float."

He quickly tied off the guy and made the main she~
fast to hold the boom in position. The ammunition box~
dangled just above the water, directly abeam. He ran fo~
ward. It was growing light now, and the tide was at~
standstill. They had to get her off before it started to dro~
Ten or fifteen minutes at the most, he thought.

He slid the bar into a slot in the drum, and heave~
upward. The ratchet clicked, and clicked again. Just ta~
ing up the slack, he thought. *Come on, baby. You c~
do it*. The warp ran aft as rigid as iron. He took a fre~
purchase and heaved. The ratchet clicked three times~
rapid succession, and then once more, and Rae Osbor~
cried out, "Ingram! *She moved—*" Her voice broke, a~
he realized for the first time that she was crying.

They got a foot. Another foot. She stopped. He heav~
upward with his shoulder under the bar, praying the a~
chor would hold and that the warp wouldn't part. S~
came free, and moved back a few inches. Her keel's st~
dragging in the sand, he thought. But if they could get h~
back another fifteen feet they'd have it made. Sweat w~
pouring off his face. Rae Osborne was leaning back wi~
her feet braced against the deck, pulling against the wi~
lass with all her strength.

"You don't have to pull," he gasped. "Just keep~
strain."

"I know," she said brokenly, "but I can't help it."

They were gaining steadily now. Five feet of warp came over the stern. She stopped again. He put his shoulder the bar. God, he prayed, don't let her hang up now. st a few more feet. Just a few more— She came free. e moved ten feet. Fifteen. The line began to come in oothly, almost easily. The keel was off the sand now, d she was completely afloat. He dropped the bar and n aft. Jumping down into the cockpit, he caught the rp and hauled. She was moving freely, and they could ll her faster without the windlass as long as they kept r momentum alive. Rae Osborne ran back and joined n. They pulled side by side, gasping for breath, while coil of dripping nylon grew larger in the cockpit. en they were in the channel, with at least six feet of ter under the keel. The warp began to lead down- rd. He took a turn and a hitch around the cleat, and od up.

Rae Osborne straightened, and stood looking at him th tears streaming down her face. She brushed at them th her hand, and laughed, but her voice broke and she rted to cry again. "Don't mind me," she said in a very all voice. "I'm just having the hysterics you promised ." Then she was in his arms, and he was kissing her the mouth and throat and all over the tear-streaked e. They both began to laugh, somewhat crazily, and lapsed on the cockpit seat.

"Ingram, you did it! You're wonderful."

"*We* did it," he corrected.

"Was I any help?"

"You don't think I could have done it alone, do you?"

"What do we do now?"

"Hold her here until the tide starts to ebb, and then her drift down this channel until we're at least out range of Morrison and his rifle. Then we'll have to it for a breeze to sail her off the Bank. We've got no trol over her at all this way, and we might go aground in."

"Good Lord! I forgot all about Morrison. Why do you pose he didn't shoot at us when he saw we were get- g away?"

133

"He may not know it yet," Ingram said. "He must hav[e] gone to sleep. I just hope he doesn't wake up until w[e] get farther away." He reached for the glasses and focuse[d] them on the sand spit, but the light was still too poor [to] see anything at that distance. He could be asleep behin[d] the boxes, anyway.

"What'll happen to him now?" she asked.

"He's got water. He'll be all right until the Coa[st] Guard can send a boat or plane down to pick him up."

They sat and rested, suddenly aware now with the r[e]lease of tension just how near complete exhaustion the[y] were. "Do you realize," she asked, "that it was only tw[o] days ago, almost to the hour, that we landed out here?"

He shook his head. "It's not possible."

The schooner swung around. The tide was beginning [to] ebb. There was enough light now to judge the water['s] depth with some degree of safety. He heaved up the a[n]chor and let her drift slowly seaward, watching the wat[er] depth with some degree of safety. He heaved up the a[n]chor again, gave her enough scope to hold, and took t[he] warp forward so she would lie bow to the tide in t[he] normal manner. He heaved the lead. "Fifteen feet," h[e] said. "and plenty of water on all sides. We're at least [a] half mile from him now, so he won't even bother [to] shoot. We'll wait here till we get a breeze, and in t[he] meantime I'll start cleaning out the bilge so we can pum[p] that gas overboard."

The sun was just coming up. She looked around, a[nd] sighed, almost in wonder. "I just can't seem to grasp t[he] fact we're off that sand bar at last."

Something fell below in the cabin. It sounded [as] though books were sliding out of the rack because of t[he] schooner's extreme list to port. "I'll take care of it," I[n]gram said. "I want to open the rest of those porthole[s] anyway."

He went down the ladder. The light below was qui[te] good now, and he could see the lake of gasoline exten[d]ing up out of the bilge along the port side for almost t[he] full length of the cabin. He thought it was higher than [it] had seemed in the dark; the chances were that water ha[d] come in through some of Morrison's bullet holes and t[he]

134

s was floating on top of it. Well, no more could come while she was over on her side, and he could take re of it as soon as he cleared the litter out of the bilge. he fumes were sickening. Two books had fallen out of rack and were lying in the edge of the gasoline near the rward end of the cabin. He picked them up and tossed em onto a bunk.

"Youse is a good boy, Herman," a voice said behind m. "I knew all the time you could do it."

He whirled. Morrison was leaning against the ladder, ked except for a pair of shorts. He had a cigarette ngling from the corner of his mouth, a pack of them his left hand, and a large kitchen match in his right, head poised under his thumbnail. He grinned, and ssed the pack. "Smoke?"

12

gram let them fall into the gasoline. It's all been for thing, he thought, in some detached and icy calm that s beyond terror. That's exactly the spot he was stand-g in that other morning three hundred years ago, and thing has changed at all except he's wearing a little s and he's got a match in his hand instead of a Brown-g Automatic Rifle. Maybe there is no way you can feat him; he's a natural force of some kind. He's wait-g for me to panic, to scream *Don't strike that match.* ell, maybe I will; I don't know.

He had to say something, but he was afraid his voice uld crack. If he ever knows how near the edge I am, thought, we've had it. And if he really *is* insane, we've d it anyway, but the only thing to do is try to wait him t. He pushed the cigarettes out of the gasoline with his t, reached down, and tossed them onto the bunk. Then heard Rae Osborne cry out. She's even in the same place, he thought. Morrison didn't bother to look up th[e] hatch; he merely took a step up the inclined deck to sta[r]board so as to be out from under it. Then he chuckle[d]

"The gun, Herman."

Ingram shook his head. Maybe he could speak no[w] At least he had to try. "When did you get aboard?" h[e] asked. It seemed to sound all right.

"When you both ran back here to pull on the rope, Morrison replied. "I ducked into that front cabin. Abo[ut] that gun, Herman. I don't know whether you ever made [a] study of 'em, but when you shoot one, some of the grai[ns] of powder that're still burning come out behind th[e] slug—"

"Yes," Ingram said. "I know about that. Excuse me—[" He raised his voice just slightly, and addressed the top [of] the ladder. "Rae, there's a life ring on either side of th[e] cockpit. Take one and go forward, right to the bow. An[d] remember to go upstream, against the tide."

Morrison shook his head. "You're a pretty hard bo[y,] Herman, but not that hard. Pass the gun over, and let[']s get started to Cuba. It's only a hundred miles. You lan[d] me—"

"Sure," Ingram said. "We land you, and then we sa[il] the boat back to Key West, the same way we were goin[g] to sail it back from Bahía San Felipe. As far as you'[re] concerned, I've had it, Morrison. I'm up to here. G[o] ahead and strike your match."

Morrison's eyes were cold. "You think I won't?"

"I don't know," Ingram replied. "But if you do, don['t] forget I'll be the lucky one. I've got the gun."

He saw that penetrate. Silence tightened its grip o[n] the scene. The *Dragoon* rocked gently on some remna[nt] of surge running in from the Santaren Channel and [a] little wave of gasoline slapped against the bulkhead a[nd] ran back to spread itself up across the steep incline of th[e] cabin sole. He has to go with the bluff, Ingram though[t,] we've probably got less than a minute left before th[e] fumes get us, and he knows he can't take the gun awa[y] from me and get out of here alive. It would take long[er] than that. One of us has to crack.

He saw movement then in the hatch. A hand ha[d]

ached in and lifted the fire extinguisher from its bracket
 the bulkhead near the ladder, and was pointing it—
uite steadily, he thought—down into the cabin. Some-
ing came up in his throat, and he didn't know whether
 was going to laugh or cry. She might as well try to
ut out hell with a damp Kleenex, but she was ready to
ckle it.

"I don't think you read me, Herman," Morrison said.
n a deal like this, you've got to consider who has the
ost to lose. Now, you take you and Mama-san—"

Ingram breathed softly. *He's not quite so sure now,*
 thought; when he has to drive home his point by ex-
aining the obvious. "Who'd you kill in Florida?" he
ked. "Was it Ives?"

Morrison studied the match in his hand, and then
oked across at him with a very cold smile. "That's a
od question, Herman. It was a cop."

Ingram felt the dark fingers of panic reaching for him,
d Barney's flaming figure began to beat against the
ter defenses of his mind. Here we go, he thought. Then,
ddenly, it was gone, and he was all right again; maybe
e accumulated hours of bilge-diving in gasoline had
rned him some sort of immunization against horror so
at it no longer had the power to break him. He could
el himself growing drunk on the fumes, however, and
ew that time was growing very short. *Wait him out,*
 told himself. "What happened to Ives?" he asked.

Morrison grinned. "So you figured that out?"

"Sure."

Everything seemed to be growing wine-colored, as if
 were late afternoon. And he noticed now that the fire
tinguisher no longer showed in the hatch. Rae Osborne
d moved. Maybe she had fainted.

"This deputy sheriff stopped us on a back-country road
st after we got the guns in the truck," Morrison went
. "I think all he wanted was to give us a ticket because
e of the tail lights was out, but that stupid Ives pan-
ed and shot at him. The cop killed Ives, and I got
e cop. I had to then. We dumped 'em out in the swamp
d took all of Ives' identification so they couldn't trace
m back to us, but if he had a record they've probably

137

got him made by now. So you figure out whether I'm going back or not."

Ingram saw the nozzle of the fire extinguisher then at the porthole just above and to the right of Morrison's head. So that's where she went, he thought dully, as the cabin began to eddy slowly around him in the gathering darkness.

Morrison flourished the hand holding the match. "You call it, Herman. Toss me the gun, or up we go. And I mean now."

The stream from the fire extinguisher hit his hand, and as the soggy and harmless match dropped from it and he turned, he caught the carbon tetrachloride full in the face. He threw up an arm to cover his eyes. Ingram leaped, swinging the .45. He felt the shock as it connected with the side of Morrison's head, and they were both falling with Morrison on top of him. He clawed his way out from under the inert mass and tried to climb to his feet. His legs gave way under him and he fell, but one of his outstretched arms was across the bottom rung of the ladder. It was all dark now. He held his breath and started up. Don't breathe till you're off the ladder, he told himself. You'll fall back. It's the first breath of fresh air that knocks you out. Don't breathe—

He felt a pair of arms catch him and pull him forward into the cockpit just as he fell.

Late the following afternoon, the *Dragoon,* under all working canvas, lay over gently on the starboard tack in a light northeasterly breeze as she stood up the Santaren Channel toward the coast of Florida. The breeze had come up shortly after ten that morning, and the treacherous sand bars and pastel blues and greens of the Great Bahama Bank were already over the horizon to starboard and astern as their course gradually took them farther offshore into the comforting indigo and the ageless heave and surge of deep water. Ingram was dead tired, but content. It had been a period of back-breaking labor at the pump, but there had been time for a little sleep and a bath and a shave. He stood now on the foredeck and took a quick look at the trim of the sails and the ventilating

138

sh-up he had rigged. Everything was drawing beautifully.
e ducked down the forward hatch, squeezing past the
nvas throat of the wind chute. The air was sweet below.

Morrison lay in one of the bunks in the forward cabin
ith the air from the ventilator washing over him. His
ands and feet were tied, and made fast to the head and
e foot of the bunk. There were bad rope burns under
s arms and across the naked chest from the sling and the
ckle they'd rigged to get him up the hatch into the
ckpit, and a lump on the side of his head, but otherwise
was all right. After the gasoline was overboard and the
ntilator rigged, they'd brought him back down here.
e lay now with his eyes closed. Ingram didn't know
hether he was asleep or merely faking it. He leaner over
e bunk and checked his hands and feet for circulation.
hey were warm, and a healthy flesh color; the ropes
ere all right.

"Get lost, Herman," Morrison said, without opening
s eyes.

Ingram looked down at him in the waning light of
ternoon. There was no feeling about him at all any
ore—no hatred, nothing. "Who was the man that
owned? He have any name besides Herman?"

The lips scarcely moved in the big, rugged face with
brown splotches of freckles. "Reefers."

"Reefers what?"

"Hell, I don't know. Judson, Jensen—something like
at. Everybody just called him Reefers. He smoked 'em."

"Marijuana?"

"Sure. Tea. Pod, the Beats call it."

"Did you know he used heroin?"

"No. So that's the reason he kept his shirt on all the
ne."

"I guess so," Ingram said. "You want to go to the
ad?"

"No. Get lost, will you?"

"If you ditched all of Ives' identification, why'd you let
eefers keep his watch?"

"I didn't know the dumb clown had it. He must have
pt it in his pocket."

Ingram walked back through the galley and the pas-

sageway to the large after cabin. The air was fresh an
clean here too, with good circulation from the ventilate
forward and no odor of gasoline at all. Since pumpir
the last of it overboard shortly before noon yesterds
they'd flooded the bilges twice with sea water and pumpe
them out. Then he'd used fifty gallons of fresh water ar
a half case of soap powder to scrub down the cabin ar
engine compartment, everything the gasoline had touche
letting the soapy water run into the bilge and pumping
overboard. They were taking some sea water through
few bullet holes below water line, but a few minutes
the pump every four hours took care of it.

He stepped quietly up the first two rungs of the ladd
and his eyes softened as he paused with his head ju
above the level of the hatch. She hadn't seen him. Sh
was perched on the helmsman's seat in back of tl
wheel, wearing a pair of his khaki trousers rolled up
the knees and gathered in folds about the slender wai
with a piece of line, and one of his shirts with the sleev
rolled up. Her mouth was nicely painted, but the taw
hair was wind-blown, and there was an expression of pu
joy on her face. Or maybe you'd call it half an expre
sion, he mused with tender humor. Some of the swellir
was gone from the eye now, but it still retained all i
startling and chromatic grandeur with its blues and pu
ples splashed so spectacularly against the blonde ar
handsome face.

She looked happily around the sea for a moment, ar
when her eyes returned to the binnacle he could tell sl
was off course. Her face took on the sudden and furio
concentration of a child's and her tongue protruded fro
the corner of her mouth as she wrestled with the proble
of which way to turn the wheel. He could almost he:
her repeating to herself: *Don't try to move the compas
move the lubber-line. Don't try to move the compas
move the lubber-line.*

He grinned, erased it from his face, and said stern
"How's your course, Mate?"

She glanced up at him, her face alight. "I'm off five d
grees to—to— Oh, the devil." She gave up and pointe
to windward. "That way. That's not too bad, is it?"

140

He smiled. "Not too bad, considering we don't even now whether the compass is within ten degrees of being ght. Anyway, I wouldn't worry about it. From a hun- ed miles out, North America's a pretty big target."

He came up the ladder and sat down beside her. "We ould raise Miami sometime after daylight in the morn- g if this breeze holds."

"I'm not in any hurry," she said. "Are you?"

"No."

She glanced up at the great curving expanse of white cron cutting across the sky. A little dollop of spray ew back and spatted against the cushions. "How long s this been going on?" she asked.

"Several thousand years," he replied.

They fell silent for a moment. Then he asked, "You ant me to take it for a while?"

She shook her head. "No. Just watch, and tell me en I do something wrong." She brought the wheel up couple of spokes. "Ingram?"

He turned. She was staring fixedly, and a little self- nsciously, into the binnacle. "What?" he asked.

"Do you have any great desire to get rich?"

"Not particularly," he said.

"Could two people sail this boat? Very far, I mean?"

"Hmmm. Under some circumstances. But most of the e they'd have their hands full."

"But what about two people who'd just as soon have ir hands full of each other, at least a good part of the e?"

"I'd recommend something a little smaller. Say a forty- forty-five-foot ketch. Why?"

"That would still be large enough for the charter busi- ss?"

"Sure." He grinned. "At least, for somebody who ln't care whether he got rich or not."

She continued to stare at the compass. "Well, say you ew two people like that who had a forty-five-foot ketch. d they wanted to go in the charter business—maybe Nassau—but one of them didn't know anything about ats and sailing at all. Wouldn't you think the ideal

141

solution would be for them to sail the boat from Miami to Nassau so this second party could learn all about it?

He gave her a thoughtful glance, wondering what she was up to. "Sure," he said. "It's at least a hundred and fifty miles, and if this hypothetical joker of yours is as brilliant as he is lovely—"

"I was thinking of another route. By way of the India Ocean."

"What?"

"That's the reason I asked you if you really cared much about making money. I don't think you do. I don't either."

"It'd take two or three years."

She removed her attention from the binnacle long enough to give him a delighted, low-comedy leer. " know. I know."

He started to reach for her.

"Hands off, sailor. I'm at the wheel. And I want t talk to you."

"All right. But talk fast, Mate."

"We've kicked this around quite a bit already. I mean how adult we are and how we've got sense enough t know that people don't fall in love with each other i four days, and you've told me at least six times that I'v seen you only in your own special environment, doing th things you do best, and all the rest of that wisdom-of-the ages routine, and how we have to be sensible, and so o But I also know what you told me when you were comin to here in the cockpit yesterday with your head in m lap, trying to get your breath through an overcast of larg soggy blonde. You said you loved me. And, in betwee raising the mean annual rainfall of the Bahamas, that wa what I was telling you. But we're going to be sensib about it, aren't we?"

"Yes. I think so. Or I mean, I did think so."

She went on, still staring intently into the binnacl "You bet we're going to be sensible, Ingram. This wa When we get into Miami, I'm going back to my ow environment, and take a long, slow look at it—as yo suggested—while you do another of these technical job you never let me pay you for. I want you to put th

142

agoon in shipyard, have her replanked in those places
ı said she needed it, overhauled, and repainted, and
:n sell her. You'll have my power of attorney. Then
ı buy a forty- or forty-five-foot ketch—"

"Sure, but—"

"All right, all right, if you insist on being stuffy about
you can pay half of it. But let me finish. You put this
:ond boat in the shipyard and have everything done to
:hat has to be done to put it in absolutely perfect con-
ion. And if you keep watching the shipyard gate, some
ernoon you're going to see a car with Texas license
.tes pull up in front of it and stop. Inside will be a big
ling blonde with a big fading black eye, and if you hap-
1 to be close to the car door when it opens you're going
think somebody just dynamited a log-jam of blondes
newhere upriver without warning the settlers to get
:—"

He still had one knee against the wheel even after they
:h forgot about it, and after a long time when he had
sed his lips from hers just to look at her again he be-
ne conscious at last of the rattle of slides against the
cks and the rolling slap of canvas as the *Dragoon* came
into the wind. "Mate, I think you're off course."

She drew a finger tip very thoughtfully along the line of
jaw. "Don't you believe it, Skipper. Don't believe it
a minute."

THE INCREDIBLE STORY
OF A MAGNIFICENT REBEL
WHO WOULD LIVE FREE...
OR NOT AT ALL!

THE INTERNATIONAL BEST SELLER
NOW A POCKET BOOK

"A tale of adventure such as few of us could ever imagin
far less survive."—Book-of-the-Month Club News

▼ AT YOUR BOOKSTORE OR MAIL THE COUPON BELOW